GRASS
AND
SKY

by Lisa Rowe Fraustino

ORCHARD BOOKS · NEW YORK

Orchard Books
95 Madison Avenue
New York, NY 10016

Manufactured in the United States of America
✪ Printed on recycled paper
Book design by Rosanne Kakos-Main

10 9 8 7 6 5 4 3 2 1

The text of this book is set in 12 point Book Antiqua.

Library of Congress Cataloging-in-Publication Data
Fraustino, Lisa Rowe.
Grass and sky / by Lisa Rowe Fraustino.
p. cm.
Summary: Eleven-year-old Timmi untangles family secrets and gets to know the grandfather her parents have "protected" her from when they visit him in the Maine woods.
ISBN 0-531-06823-4. — ISBN 0-531-08673-9 (lib. bdg.)
[1. Grandfathers—Fiction. 2. Families—Fiction.] I. Title.
PZ7.F8655Gr 1994
[Fic]—dc20
93-25210

*To my parents,
Buddy and Carole Rowe,
who gave me the grass and sky*

Dear Grampy
This is wens~~daoa~~bay.
It was Jim bay.
I love Jim bay
Jim is my favorite tim
in all ov first grade.
I know how to spel Jim.
Daddys name is Jim.
Mama se~~xb~~ to spel
favorite FAVORITE.
I spelt all the rest
all dy myself.
Can you vizet me
TOMORROW
Love
Timmi Lafler

1

*B*efore I even got my *d*'s and *b*'s straight, I used to write letters to Grampy Lafler. I'd ask Mama how to spell the words I didn't know. Then I'd seal the letter in an envelope, address it "To Grampy in Maine," draw a picture of the Stars and Stripes in the top right-hand corner, and drop the envelope in the mailbox.

Finally Mama caught on to me and explained about zip codes and paid-for stamps. Then I wrote more letters to Grampy. He still didn't write back.

"Why, why, why!" I cried to Mama one day after the mail came with nothing for me.

She shrugged and pulled me close. "I know he cares about you, Timmi. Maybe he's too busy to write."

No sense writing to someone who's too busy to write back. I stopped when I was nine, even though he was my only living grandparent and I wanted to know him so much that my throat hurt when I thought about him.

We never visited Grampy, and Grampy never visited us. "Is there some awful reason why we can't see him?" I'd ask. "Does he have a deathly contagious disease or something?"

*No time, too far, when your sister's a little older—*excuses, excuses, excuses.

The only one in our family who ever went to stay in the Maine woods with Grampy was our dog, Charlie, because my little brat sister was allergic to him. "Charlie was here first. It's Rebecca you should be sending into exile," I told my parents, but they just said, "We'll miss him too, honey," and waved good-bye to the train he was on.

After that I nagged Mama and Daddy to tell me why we never visited Charlie.

When I complained to my best friend, Samantha Mackinder, she said, "At least you have grand*parents.*" She didn't just mean Mama and Daddy are great and look like grandparents (which explains the demise of my other three—old age). Samantha's dad died in an accident, so I felt lucky then to have Mama and Daddy.

Well, last summer, finally, at long last, we visited Grampy Lafler. But the reunion wasn't the happy day I'd always imagined.

In June, when Daddy announced we were going to Grampy's for two weeks, I whooped a cheer. But then he said, "The first two weeks in July," and I said, "Whoa, Daddy." The best two weeks of baseball season, stuck in the boonies? I'd rather be benched—that's how much I love baseball. Summers I can't think of much else, except for my next issue of *Ellery Queen's Mystery Magazine*.

"We can't go then!" I told him. "I'm pitching against Buddy Loring in the first game of the Independence Day Tourney!"

"We can't put it off, Timmi," said Mama. "You can strike out Buddy when we get back to Scranton. This is the only time that's good for your grandfather."

"I'll stay home alone, then," I said. "I'm almost twelve."

"No way!" my parents chimed. They wouldn't even change their minds when Coach begged them to let me stay with his family.

I was extra infuriated, let me tell you. All those years with no Grampy, and all of a sudden we had to go to Fish Lake?

"This is suspicious," I said. "There must be some sort of conspiracy going on. A Buddy Loring sort."

Daddy laughed and said, "You've been reading too many mysteries."

"So explain why I have to see Grampy next week instead of seeing Buddy humiliate himself!"

"You'll see for yourself soon enough," said Daddy.

A week later, we turned onto Grampy's "driveway," as Daddy called it. It was actually a logging road—twenty-three miles of packed dust and potholes. Its official name was The Road. The Cow Path, more like. We had to stop the car and wait like heifers for the security guard to open the gate.

When Daddy was a kid, he and his parents lived in a real town, Dexter, during the school year. They spent summers at their "camp" on Fish Lake, where Grampy now lived year-round. It was so far away from any town that he went to pick up his mail and groceries just once a week.

At Grampy's place there was no electricity, no phone, no TV. Everything the least bit civilized used gas: the lights, the stove, even the hot water. No wonder they called it *camp*. But only after the six-hundred-and-some-odd–mile drive from Pennsylvania did Daddy reveal these facts. Suspicious. It struck me how little I knew about him growing up. Why didn't he ever talk about it?

Daddy saw my disgusted expression in the rearview mirror. "Consider yourself lucky, Timmi," he said. "When I was your age, we had kerosene lamps. We took a bath in the lake, which was mighty cold in the morning! *And*"—snicker snicker—"we went to the bathroom in an outhouse with no running water. We were lucky if we had toilet tissue. Whenever Grampy came back from the outhouse, he'd act all excited. 'Gotta go to town, Mother,' he'd say. 'I used the last page of the Sears catalog!' A few minutes later he'd jump up and run toward the door, yelling, 'I fergut to flush the toilet!' "

Nobody laughed.

"Get it? There's no flush in an outhouse," Daddy explained. "Yup, your grandfather always was a practical joker."

Daddy laughed, but I hadn't noticed anything funny about the story. "If this place doesn't have a flush, I'm going home right this minute even if I have to walk," I told him. Either that or hold it in for two weeks, which nobody can do.

"Timmi, calm down. The camp has running water and a regular bathroom now," Mama said. "No outhouse."

The car turned through a gap in the endless pines. "Here we are," Daddy said. We crunched to a stop beside an old brown Jeep with a banged-up white license plate that said GOFISH.

Daddy leaned back and took a deep breath. "Smells just the way I remember it." He sounded happier than I'd expected. One of his old excuses for not visiting Grampy was, "The most exciting thing to do there is watch birds build nests."

Daddy likes the city. He says there's more privacy in a crowd because nobody knows each other.

I sniffed. The air smelled like a combination of Christmas trees and springtime. Birds sang, trees creaked gently, the wind seemed to hum. A dog bayed. Charlie! But I hardly recognized the cloudy-eyed beagle that trotted slowly from the woods and stood outside Rebecca's window, growling and drooling. Rebecca screamed, of course, and dived over the seat into Mama's lap.

Daddy opened his door and made a kissy sound. "Here, Charlie! Here, boy!"

The dog cocked his head to listen. Then, suddenly, he yapped, ran around the car, and jumped up against Daddy's knees. Charlie's stubby tail wagged so fast, it looked like the blade of a fan. Now, that was the spunky dog I used to know. His tail wagging reminded me of the only time I remembered seeing Grampy, the day Mama and my new baby sister came home from the hospital.

As soon as I stepped off the bus from kindergarten, I heard a deep voice hollering slurry words in the kitchen. I ran up the driveway. Daddy was waiting in the doorway and scooched so I could run straight into a hug. Mama sat at the kitchen table, nursing Rebecca. A thin man, old, with sunken-in, unshaven cheeks, leaned against the counter. Charlie sat drumming the floor with his tail stub.

"Timothea! Give Grampy a hug!" Grinning, the man lunged toward me, and I ran to huddle under Mama's arm. That's all I remembered.

Kneeling next to the Jeep, Daddy giggled like a kid and let the dog lap his face. *My father* actually had tears in his eyes! "You're still here!" Daddy's voice was raspy. "I can't believe it. I thought you'd be in beagle heaven by now."

"A dog nevuh forgets his first mastuh," a drawn-out voice boomed from the path at the front of the clearing.

That time when I was little, Grampy had seemed to tower over us all. Now, when Daddy hopped up to shake his hand, Grampy stood eye-to-eye with him. Grampy had a gray, bushy beard flecked with black and white. His ghostly pale skin sagged at the neck and under the eyes. When he reached out to rub Charlie between the ears, I noticed how wrinkled and yellowed his hands were.

Daddy and his father stared at each other for a long time. I climbed out of the car, keeping my eyes on Grampy because I couldn't see Daddy's face. The old man seemed overjoyed, a big grin splitting his beard. His gray eyes turned bright, almost black.

"Well. The prodigal son returns at last," said Grampy happily, slapping Daddy on the back.

Daddy shook his head, his forehead crinkling. "Your sense of humor hasn't changed, has it, Father."

The smile faded. "I didn't mean any offense—"

Mama cleared her throat. "Hello, Jimmy!"

"Kathy!" that deep voice bellowed. "My deah! I can't tell you how good it is to see you!"

I wondered why he hadn't said anything like that to Daddy. Definitely suspicious.

Grampy moved to hug her, but Mama was holding Rebecca on her hip. Rebecca let a scream out of her that you could have heard back at the Cow Path gate. "I want to go home!" she howled, and burst into tears. She buried her face in Mama's neck. Mama looked embarrassed.

"No mind, little shy boots," Grampy said. "Blue Eyes heah will come around." He squeezed Rebecca's sneaker toe.

I wondered if that made me Brown Eyes, but when he looked at me he said, "So, this is Timothea."

That very moment I knew I wasn't going to like him. He smiled at me like Mama and Daddy do when I make them proud—a regular doting grandfather. He had no right to look at me like that! You can't care that much about someone you don't know. Faking out is for baseball, not for families.

"No, this is Timmi," I said, and turned to wrestle with Charlie.

I didn't much like Grampy or being boonied, but a thrill trickled through me when I saw the gigantic maple tree at the head of the path to camp. Flowing letters were carved into the trunk: *Camp Timothea*. The name I inherited from Grammy Lafler could actually be pretty!

Daddy often stares at the old black-and-white photograph of Grammy that hangs in our hall. Sometimes (I suspect) he even cries. Looking at that dimply babyish face and those sparkling eyes in the picture, I wonder how she could ever die.

"God rest her. . . ." Grampy sounded so sad, I twirled to look at him. He turned away.

A strange moan, shrill and mournful, cried out in the distance. "What's that," I said, "the ghost of Fish Lake?"

"Hmp. A loon's all. Camp's thisaway," said Grampy, pointing his nose downhill.

Daddy had already loaded himself with luggage and moved along, Charlie limping at his heels. Mama followed with Rebecca on one hip and a garment bag on the other. I hoisted my suitcase up and set off. Grampy's footsteps crunched behind me. He didn't carry anything. I guess he had a hard enough time carrying himself downhill.

After one bend in the path, I stopped short to catch my breath. Fish Lake had taken it away. I'd never seen such a big, beautiful lake. The waves rippled between shiny spots of sun, and in the distance the opposite shore made a dark frame. The lake looked like a postcard, too blue—too perfect—to be real.

"Timothea, I've lived here fifty summers and then some, and it still takes my breath away," Grampy said, right behind me.

Cripes, it made me mad that Grampy could read my mind like that. And *Timothea*! I made a point of looking away from the lake. That's when I saw a tiny log cabin nestled into the trees as if it grew there.

"That the outhouse?" I said. "You flushed it lately?"

"You mean the *bunk*house? Your fathuh told you that old outhouse story? Well, I'll be jiggered!" The old man broke into laughter, choked, and bent over double, coughing. I went and tapped him on the back. Not that I cared if he laughed himself sick, but Mama and Daddy would have killed me if I let Grampy choke to death. He caught his breath and thanked me.

"I near fergut about them days. I guess prob'ly you and me's going to have a fine time togethuh, Timothea," he said, getting that fond look on his face again.

It was just like pitching low and outside to Buddy Loring, but he hits a double anyway. I meant to insult Grampy, and he got affectionate. The same guy who never cared enough to scribble a letter back to me?

I ran down the path. So far I hadn't seen any reason why we had to visit Grampy now. Or ever.

_2

*T*he path wound downhill and around the bunkhouse, then swelled open into a clearing. Right there snuggled up against the forest stood the camp, a one-story log cabin with green wooden shutters. *Prison* camp, I thought.

I was going to leave my suitcase at the door and run to the lake, but the screen was letting a mouth-watering smell out of the kitchen. No one was in the room. I followed my nose to the old-fashioned black cookstove and opened the oven. Inside sat a dirt-colored pot bubbling with beans. Beans! How could they make my mouth water? I looked around. Two loaves of bread sat rising on the counter, and next to them a long cake pan. My nose liked the looks of that.

I took a fork from the sink and cut out a bite of cake. What a smell! Like cinnamon in an apple orchard. The warm cake practically melted in my mouth. I started cutting another piece.

"Timmi, if you don't dislocate your paws from that cake right now, you're going to wish you did." Daddy stood in the doorway to the next room, looking half amused, half worried. "Grampy will cut him a fresh switch for anyone who doesn't follow the rules."

"What rules? Can't a hungry person have something to eat around here?" It was bad enough to *be* there. But to have to follow rules you didn't even know about!

"Certainly. You can eat all you want at dinnertime." Daddy came over and peered down at the cake pan. "Is it good? It smells fantastic."

I jabbed the piece I had been cutting out. "It's delicious. Taste," I said, and shoved it in his face.

Daddy looked around, sly as Ellery Queen swiping evidence. He opened his mouth, and I plopped the cake in. He mm-mmed and yummed like you do when your sweet tooth gets fed.

Then a growly-barky noise came in through the

screen door. It wasn't Charlie, either. Grampy had finally made it downhill. He came in and leaned against the wall, his face tired and pained.

"Some things nevuh change, eh, Jimbo?"

Jimbo! Daddy's boss and Mama are allowed to call him Jim, but everyone else has to call him James, or else. Whenever someone gets familiar and calls him Jimmy, Daddy bristles up like a cat in dog country.

I laughed. Jimbo sounded funny. And I thought Daddy was going to give it to Grampy.

Actually, Daddy sort of gave it to me. "What's so funny, young lady?" he yelled. "Get out of here, before I make me a switch." His voice had a drawl I'd never heard in it before, like Grampy's.

Weird. The only kind of switch I knew about was the kind you use to turn lights on. But I had an idea it wasn't anything fun. I went looking for Mama, who's good to hide behind, and hoped to find the facilities along the way.

The next room was the living room. It had a stone fireplace beside the door to the kitchen. There wasn't any couch, just recliners, armchairs, and rockers gathered around a lobster trap with a glass tabletop. A puzzle was sprawled out on it.

I like puzzles, so I picked up the box. I had to laugh. Just a hundred pieces! It was a picture of different-colored houses all over the place, no grass and sky. I'd do it in three minutes, easy. Grampy had to be pretty dim to enjoy a simple puzzle like that. And a real quitter to leave it undone. Nobody likes quitters, except I'd love it if Buddy Loring would quit trying to prove I'm a boy. He can't stand getting struck out, especially by someone with a ponytail and fingernails.

Off to the side was a dark room where I saw the outline of a tub, the kind with a rounded bottom and four legs like claws. I went in and was pleased to see a lump that looked like a real *flushing* flush.

The light switch wasn't next to the door, and I didn't have time to grope around for it. I closed the door behind me and flew to do what I had to do. Then I groped around to find the toilet paper. But *no*. It wasn't on the wall, on the flush tank, or on the floor within my reach.

This was serious. I couldn't get up to find the

lights, or I'd really be in a mess. The room didn't have a window, which ordinarily would thrill me, since it would be impossible for half the Little League to play Peeping Tom and see for themselves whether Buddy has a case. But this once I would have loved a bathroom window to put a little light on the subject.

I was ready to call for help (Grampy to the rescue—how humiliating!) when I nudged a booklet stuck behind the toilet bowl. Of course I realized it might be a Sears catalog, but I had no choice. I did the necessary. Thank goodness the toilet flushed.

I practically ran out of that bathroom and took the booklet along just to see if I'd flushed anything important or embarrassing. It wasn't a catalog, just some magazine called *Grapevine*.

A terrible thought came to me. Maybe Grampy didn't buy toilet paper, and I'd be stuck scraping myself with that scratchy *Grapevine* for two weeks. It made me so mad, I stormed out to the screened-in porch, where I'd been hearing Mama's and Rebecca's voices jabbering away while I was groping for toilet paper.

"I've had it! I've had it up to here!" I jumped

up to tinkle the wind chimes dangling from the ceiling. "No way am I staying here with this . . . this . . . this *cave man*!"

Mama was sitting on a porch swing, reading some Disney version of *Winnie-the-Pooh* to Rebecca. I could have been dying, and Mama just calmly looked up and said, "Pardon me?"

"Mama!" Rebecca yowled. "It's time for Tigger to say—"

"Aaaarrrrhhhh!" I cut in. "I don't believe this! I've just been through the most traumatic experience of my entire twelve years, and you're talking about Tigger!"

"You're only eleven," said Rebecca.

"Is there something wrong?" Mama asked me, but patting Rebecca's cheek.

"If that stupid stone-age bathroom had a light switch next to the door, I wouldn't have had to use a *catalog* instead of *toilet paper,* and if Daddy didn't threaten to use a switch on me, I would have *asked* where the bathroom was, and then maybe someone would have told me where to find the light switch and toilet paper." There was more to say, but I had to stop and breathe.

"Let's read the part where Tigger sings the

song," Rebecca said. "It goes, 'The wonderful thing about—'"

"Mama!" I screamed. "Please!"

I can't believe how she lets Rebecca act. Every time we go grocery shopping, Rebecca begs *canIcanIcanI* and leaves the store with loot galore. I, on the other hand, might ask, very politely, for one box of cereal with baseball cards inside, and Mama says, "For heaven's sake, Timmi, act your age."

"Rebecca, please help your father set the dinner table," Mama said now. My sister hadn't caught on yet that stuff like table setting and dish washing wasn't fun. She ran inside.

Mama folded her arms across her chest. "Now. Timmi. Why did your father threaten to use the switch on you?"

"What's a switch?"

"I asked first."

"Grampy called him Jimbo, and I laughed," I told her.

"Ah-ha. Now I see," said Mama. "Well, a switch, the way your father meant it, is a wiry tree limb that hurts like heck when snapped against the backs of your legs."

I winced at the thought of it. "Is that . . . did Daddy . . . ?"

Mama nodded. "When your father was a child, many parents felt that physical punishment was the only way to make children behave. Spare the rod and spoil the child, they said. Things are different now."

I nodded, remembering the saying from history class. "Phew. I'm glad it's all right to be spoiled now."

"By the way," Mama said, "Grampy keeps the toilet paper in a coffee can under the sink so the mice and squirrels won't get it. An old habit from the outhouse days."

It figured.

"Suppuh!" called Grampy. Mama and I joined the others at the round table in the kitchen.

Those baked beans tasted surprisingly good. I wolfed down one helping, then plunged the serving spoon into the bean pot for seconds.

"Glad you like my beans, Timothea!" boomed Grampy. "They take all day to bake."

I dropped the spoon back into the pot. "On second thought . . . ," I said, taking a thick slice of bread. Mama makes better bread than any bakery.

But this bread was the best, warm and yeasty. On my last gobble, I noticed Grampy watching me, cockier than Lydia Smart when she was the first kid in fifth grade to really need a bra.

"That's sourdough bread. I'll teach you how to make it if you like, Timothea."

The sourdough suddenly soured my stomach—and cripes, *Timothea* again. When Mama elbowed my ribs, I said, "Uh, thanks, but I don't bake."

After dinner, Mama went to clean the dust out of the bunkhouse and make an allergy-proof bed for Rebecca. Dust and other allergens can settle in the strangest places. Once Rebecca used a stuffed animal as a pillow at somebody's house, and she had an asthma attack in the middle of the night. Ever since then, Mama's been a fanatic about where Rebecca sleeps.

The rest of us went to sit on the screened-in porch.

"So," Grampy said to Daddy, "you planning on going to that big high-school reunion in Dextuh this weekend? You ain't seen your old buddies in, what, twenty-five years?" (Grampy said Dext*uh*, but the green signs along I-95 said Dext*er*.)

Daddy's face squinched, a wish behind a wince. "I thought about going, but the reunion events aren't really for families, and I'd rather not leave the girls over the weekend."

Thank goodness!

Grampy shook his head disapprovingly. "You mean to tell me you ain't going to see yourself inducted into that Hall of Local Fame they've cooked up? I've been looking forward to getting acquainted with the girls here while you and Kathy go."

"Fame? Daddy? For what?" I said.

"Your fathuh was only the best point guard in the history of Dextuh High basketball," Grampy gloated.

Daddy laughed and said, "I don't think so. Thanks anyway."

I was glad he and Mama weren't going and leaving us girls with Grampy, but you wouldn't catch me missing it if it was *my* fame. I felt puffy with pride. My father, the best! He'd told me stories about his old sports days, but he never bragged.

"Well, suit yuhself," Grampy grunted out. He reached down to rub Charlie between the ears.

For a while nobody broke the silence, and I settled into the peacefulness. Rebecca and I swish-swished on the porch swing. The crickets sounded like a concert of violins. A frog made a noise like a gong. Then a loud slap noise made me jump.

"Gotcha, you bloody mosquito!" cried Daddy. He displayed a black speck between his fingers. "This ought to replace the chickadee as Maine's state bird." On his upper arm a red mark spread out like a hand. He rubbed it. "The North Woods and I just don't seem to get along."

Grampy snickered, shaking his head, still staring out across the water. But when he spoke, he wasn't laughing. "No. I guess not. I'm sorry."

The porch felt tense right then, like that terrible moment before you let the pitch go with a count of three and two. Daddy's lips squeezed into a thin line. He clenched and unclenched his fists, then cracked his knuckles. Grampy took a pipe from an ashtray, looked into the bowl for a moment, then put the stem to his lips. Slowly, he reached into his pants pocket and pulled out a square silver lighter. It clicked open. Grampy lit the pipe. A cloud of smoke rose over his head.

Rebecca and I looked at each other, then at Grampy, then at Daddy, then at Grampy. Daddy's mouth froze open like a knothole in a petrified forest. The smoke cloud grew. Rebecca coughed a little.

"How can you smoke around Rebecca when you know she has allergies!" I yelled, glowering at Grampy's back. Smoke is her worst allergy. It gives her an asthma attack. And if her asthma gets too bad, she has to go to the hospital. I could just see us rushing Rebecca to the hospital over twenty-three miles of potholes.

Grampy turned quickly, looking disturbed. "I'm sorry. . . . I . . . was thinking. Allergies. Yes, the dog. I didn't realize about the smoke," he said. He stared down into the pipe as if he hated it.

"I'm going to the bunkhouse for my breather." Rebecca coughed her way out of the camp.

I glared at Daddy and Grampy, then ran after my sister.

3

"**Y**ou won't believe what Daddy just did," I told Mama. "Grampy practically blew smoke in Rebecca's face, and—"

"*What?*" Mama turned her head to look doubtfully at me as she swooshed a mop under the bunk.

"Well, he was smoking. Daddy didn't even say a word, just sat there with a dumb look on his face."

"Oh, I believe it." Mama sat on the double bed and dug into her handbag for Rebecca's inhaler, a small plastic thing that looks like a bent elbow. It squirts medicine for Rebecca to breathe in.

"You do?" I moved in front of Mama and stared at her. "What on earth is going on around here? Daddy's acting *weird*. Out in left field." If I didn't detest the thought of being left alone with Grampy, I'd have told her about Daddy being crazy for not going to his induction into the Hall of Local Fame.

Mama stood and handed Rebecca the inhaler. "Keep this in your sock when you're not in the bunkhouse, just in case." She watched Rebecca take a puff, load a sock, and run out. Then Mama gently tugged my ponytail.

"Just try to be patient, Timmi. Your father has a lot of feelings to sort out. You've probably noticed he and your grandfather don't get along too well."

I'd have to be deaf and blind not to notice that. Some nerve Daddy had, dragging me away from the Independence Tourney to visit someone he could hardly stand.

"But Mama, *why*? What's the big *secret*!"

She put her hands on my shoulders. "I understand why you're curious, Timmi, but the relationship between your father and grandfather is their business. Perhaps Daddy will explain when you're old enough to understand."

Right. The world's next-to-most convenient excuse, after *because I said so*.

"Honey, we're here to make some happy memories with Grampy, but he and Daddy can't change a headful of history overnight."

I pulled out from under Mama's hands, crossed my arms, and stared at her. "Why does it have to be now? Why not next month, or in six *more* years?"

She stared out the window. "As folks get older, they want to set things right in their life. Wrap it up and put a bow on it."

When Buddy Loring ruins my life, I don't waste any time getting older before I set him right. "Then what took him so long!" I cried, and suddenly felt six again, waiting under the mailbox.

"Good question." Mama turned to me, smiling her bittersweet love, and opened her arms. That smile used to make me melt like ice cream, but now it makes me nervous. I wouldn't want anyone else to see that mushy look on her face. Too embarrassing.

Still, life wouldn't be half as good without the smell of her shampoo in the morning or the sound of her voice at ball games. "Right over the plate, Timmi! You can do it!" Besides, I was feeling six again. I wrapped around her and hugged hard.

⟜

After that I ran downhill for a swim. The sun was a giant orange ball caught between two mountains. A breeze rustled through the leaves of some white birch trees leaning low over Grampy's beach. Waves slapped ashore. I walked down the dock slowly to enjoy the feel of the warm boards underfoot. Then I sat and dangled my feet in the cool, clear water.

A white dinghy bobbed on the waves, tethered to the left side of the dock. A greenish blue speedboat drummed against the right side. Along the lake's edges, a few fishing boats sat in coves. A long green canoe paddled toward Grampy's dock.

"Hullow theyuh," the boy in the canoe shouted from a few feet away. "I'm Dale Chute, from The Island. You're Timothea, right?"

With two strong, quick strokes, Dale steered the canoe toward the beach. He hopped out and pulled the canoe ashore, as quick and steady as Buddy Loring sliding into home—which surprised me. Dale Chute looked like a freckle-faced

Pillsbury Doughboy with orange food coloring spilled on his head.

"People who want to live call me Timmi. What island?" I didn't see any camps on the tiny islands scattered around. "That one?" I pointed to the largest island, about a quarter mile out.

"Nah, that's just Blueberry," Dale answered as if the whole world should know. "People picnic and camp out there sometimes. You mean you haven't heard of *The Island*?" Dale kicked off his shabby sneakers and joined me on the dock.

"I haven't had the privilege just yet," I said.

"Well, you can't see it from here. It's around that peninsula over there, about a mile away. *The Island*'s the biggest one here, a resort camp—you know, the kind rich city people pay good money to stay in."

I didn't know, but I let Dale go on.

"Mumma works there. She's the gardener and cook." He grinned and patted his stomach. "She'll invite you over to eat someday. Aren't you staying for two weeks?"

"How did you hear that?" I couldn't imagine Grampy telling anyone about a granddaughter he didn't care about enough to visit, call, or write to.

"Your grampy told me when he came to supper at The Island last week. I like him. He's taught me how to put together wicked hard puzzles."

I gulped down a laugh.

"We go fishing sometimes," Dale went on. "And he tells wicked good stories."

"Really?" Grampy was friends with *him*? I trampled the water to make bubbles churn. "How long have you known my grandfather?"

"He started visiting us this summer. Before, he was quite the hermit. Never talked to anyone on the lake." Dale took a toothpick out of his bulging pocket and chewed on the end.

"That doesn't surprise me," I said.

"It doesn't?"

I twisted around to look at the porch. Grampy sat in the shadows, rocking slowly. What a change, from quite the hermit to quite the grandfather.

Mama came running down the path with Rebecca on her shoulders. They splashed into the water, screaming and giggling. I jumped up and dived off the dock. That water was *cold*! It shocked thoughts of Grampy right out of me.

Dale stripped off his T-shirt and cannonballed in, making a mighty splash. We kept diving and splashing, and pretty soon the whitecapped water felt warm. The sun sank below the mountains, sending slices of pink across the sky. The water and the sunset made me feel like I was inside an artist's masterpiece.

Dale went ashore and shook himself dry, tossed his sneakers into the canoe, and slid it into the shadowy water. He hopped in and took off at the same time. It was *smooth*.

"Look," Mama said, pointing across the cove. Two dark heads crooked up out of the water. "Loons."

Dale cupped his hands around his mouth and belted out a scream that would have summoned a fire department if we were near one: "oo ooo OOO WOO! WOOooWOO! WOOooWOO! WOOooWOO!"

Those birds screamed right back at him.

My attempt at a loon call sounded more like a

depressed hound dog. In fact, Charlie howled at me from the porch. Grampy cackled. The loons dived underwater.

"Phooey! You scared them away," said Rebecca.

"Me, too," yelled Dale, and the canoe shot away like an arrow, leaving a narrow wake behind.

"He's weird," said Rebecca as she toweled dry. "He looks like Raggedy Andy and talks funny."

Yeah, but I was happy there was someone to talk to out there in the boonies, even if he was, well, loony.

Back on the dusky porch, I lay across the swing, wrapped in my towel. I felt tired in a peaceful sort of way. Rebecca climbed up onto the other end of the swing and curled herself like a kitten between my feet. Mama and Daddy sank into chairs.

Grampy, a dark shape in his rocker, cleared his throat, winding up for a story. "S'pose you girls nevuh heard the one about your great-grampy Lafluh going down in Maine history. True story."

Mama spat out a short laugh. "Oh, *never*," said Daddy. I knew they'd heard it—plenty of times.

"Nevuh heard it," I said. Grampy didn't even notice my new accent.

"Well," he began, rocking slow and deep, "Great-grampy lived in these woods a long time ago, when a soul couldn't buy all his food at the grocery store. One year the birds et all his garden seeds as soon as he put 'em in the ground. So he didn't have no vegetables to store for the wintuh."

"*Et* 'em, eh?" I said. Mama cleared her throat and flicked my arm with her foot, but Grampy didn't notice.

"Ayuh. Then fire got his blueberry plants just before it was time to rake 'em. So he didn't have no berries to store for the wintuh, neithuh."

"What did he eat, then?" Rebecca was worried, the sucker. Me, I was trying to decide whether to have some fun with Grampy's grammar or go to sleep.

"Hold on, the answer's part of the story," said Grampy. "Great-grampy had an icehouse to keep food cold. Well, that year the termites et his icehouse."

I opened my mouth, but Mama had her foot cocked and ready to shoot.

"And to top that off, a skunk drowned in his well. Poor old Great-grampy sure had some bad luck that year." Grampy took his pipe out of his pocket, tapped it against his ashtray, and packed it with fresh tobacco.

Daddy spoke up this time. "Uh, Father—Rebecca's asthma."

"Oh. Ayuh." Grampy put the pipe in the ashtray and took a deep breath. That made him cough before he could go on.

"Come Novembuh, Great-grampy started getting hungry. He took his double-barreled shotgun and his last bullet, and he headed for the woods, bound and determined to find some game. Walked all day without seeing so much as a field mouse. Finally he was ready to quit—oh, 'bout sundown—when he seen a red fox about fifteen or twenty yards away. Well, he took careful aim and started to pull the trigguh, when *bam*!"

He shot forward in his chair, making me jolt. Rebecca screeched a little.

"Out from behind a stump came running *anothuh* fox." Grampy seemed satisfied. He took a drink from his soda can, settled back, and rocked again.

"So what did"—I cleared my throat so he would know I hadn't fallen for his tall tale—"*Great-grampy* do? Just shoot the first fox?"

"How could Great-grampy eat a poor little fox anyway?" Rebecca sounded ready to sprout tears. Mama stretched over to squeeze her arm.

"He didn't have much choice, Blue Eyes. He had to eat what he could get," said Grampy.

"So what did he do?" I asked, yawning. Blackness had dropped around the crescent moon, a sliver just over the treetops. Daddy got up to light the gas lamps on the wall.

"What any smart person with just one bullet would do. He aimed halfway between the two foxes and pulled the trigguh."

Mama let out that short choke of a laugh again.

"If you ask me, that's pretty dumb," I said. "You can't shoot a fox if you don't aim at it."

"You can if you're Great-grampy Lafluh. He has gone down in history as the luckiest huntuh in Maine."

"Hey, you said he had *bad* luck." Rebecca got him!

"That's right, he *had* bad luck, but then his luck changed. That bullet hit a rock, split in two, and got both foxes right in the head." Grampy leaned forward and clapped his hands.

"Phoney baloney," I said.

"Ooooh, it happened, sure as bears have fleas. And not only that, the kick from the gun knocked Great-grampy into a stream flowing behind him. He hit his head on a rock and passed out—"

"You just said his bad luck was changing to good luck!" I blurted. This story had more holes in it than a backstop.

"Let me finish! When Great-grampy came to, his right hand was on a beavuh, and his left hand was on an ottuh. His pockets were so full of trout that a button popped off his pants and killed a pahtridge!" Grampy slapped his knees and put his whole weight into laughing.

Me, I didn't think it was too funny. But Mama laughed and laughed. Even Daddy tilted a smile. And Rebecca sighed.

"I'm very glad Great-grampy's luck changed," she said, "or else he might have starved like all those poor children across the ocean Mama tells us about when we don't eat our brussels sprouts."

"Oh, ayuh," Grampy said, wiping the corners

of his eyes. "Child, you warm the cockles of an old man's heart. It's a joy to have you heah." He coughed his throat clear and leaned to slap Daddy's knee. "So, did you tell Kathy about my offer to watch the girls while you get permanently famous in Dextuh?"

"What?" said Mama.

Daddy grimaced and stammered out, "Uh, I didn't exactly tell her about the reunion."

"Why on earth—? You tell me now," commanded Mama.

"I didn't tell you because I wasn't planning on going and it's no big deal, just my twenty-fifth high-school class reunion. They're hanging a plaque and some old newspaper clippings in the Town Hall's hallway of old local sports heroes."

"*Inducting* him," said Grampy with raised eyebrows. "Going to be a big to-do, even if he ain't there, I read in the *Dextuh Gazette*."

"Jim! Why didn't you tell me?" Mama looked positively offended. She'd be giving Daddy a talking-to later on, I was sure. "You know I've always wanted to meet your old classmates," Mama said. "I'd love to be there for the big to-do."

Daddy sighed. "Well, it would be nice to catch up with Chummy Bennett and Roger Edwards after all these years. But Kathy, the girls. . . ."

Well, I didn't want a guilty conscience keeping me awake all night, so instead of screaming what I was really thinking (Don't leave!), I said, "Cripes, Daddy. Rebecca and I've been walking and talking and feeding ourselves for years. I guess we'll live if you leave for one weekend."

Rebecca giggled.

Grampy winked at her and said, "Well theyuh, what's wrong with that." Then he turned to give me that doting-grandfather look again. Here we were, one big happy family.

There was plenty wrong with that. I ran to the bunkhouse and buried myself in the musty bedding of the top bunk.

4

When I woke up the next morning, my nose tingled with cold. A ceiling of shellacked wood shone down at me. I didn't know where I was. When a motorboat buzzed in the distance, I remembered Fish Lake and Grampy and his all-of-a-sudden fondness for his grandchildren.

A fat housefly settled on the log beam above my head. I swatted at it. "Rats. Missed." I stretched the morning slowness out of me.

The bed shook as Rebecca hopped out of the bottom bunk. She scampered to the double bed across the room and wriggled under the covers into the curve of Mama sleeping. Mama murmured something and wrapped her arms around Rebecca. It used to feel good curling up to Mama on lazy mornings, fitting just right. It would feel good now to join in, curl up to Daddy. But he wasn't there.

"Mama, where's Daddy?" I asked. "What time is it?"

"Early, Timmi. Go back to sleep," she mumbled, snuggling tighter to Rebecca. "Daddy went fishing."

Daddy was leaving for the holiday weekend, and he didn't even spend his last lousy morning fishing with me. That made a load of sense for a guy who didn't get along with the Maine woods! My own father was becoming more a mystery to me than any Ellery Queen character. I pulled the thick, musty-smelling quilt over my head. Sometimes it feels good to put bad feelings to sleep.

The next time I woke up, Daddy was drawing back the woven-straw window shade beside me. I winced in the blinding sunlight.

"Up 'n' at 'em, Timmi! Fresh trout for breakfast!"

The other beds were empty and already made. I wiped out the sleepy winkers, leaped from the bunk, and yanked on my favorite holey cutoffs and University of Scranton Royals T-shirt.

"Why didn't you take me fishing?" I complained on the way to the main camp.

"Sorry, sweet thing. I needed some time alone to think. But I'll be back Monday, and we—"

"What were you thinking about?" It had to be that headful of Grampy history he was hiding, and I wanted to hear some.

Daddy looked at me hard for a minute, as if he wanted to spring a terrible secret loose, but he just muttered, "Things," and looked away. Then he gushed, "Listen, Timmi, will you promise me one thing?"

I grunted yes, hoping for a secret to keep.

"It's a party weekend. If there's *any* drinking on this lake when we're gone, you'll steer clear and keep a level head?"

I rolled my eyes. "Of course, Daddy." It was the same thing he always said whenever he and Mama left me anywhere they weren't. At least this time it wasn't the complete unabridged "Evils of Alcohol" lecture he gave me and Samantha and Lydia when—just as a joke—we asked for nonalcoholic beer instead of root beer with our pizza.

In the kitchen, Mama was scrambling eggs at the stove and Rebecca was sitting at the table. Grampy was coughing and hacking in the living room, the apple scent of his pipe tobacco drifting into the kitchen. It made me mad.

"Cripes, Mama. Isn't that smoke—"

Mama pointed her spatula toward me. "That smoke isn't anywhere near Rebecca. Don't forget, this is your grandfather's home. We can't expect him to change his habits for us."

"Ain't that the truth," said Daddy, reaching around Mama to sneak a scrambled egg curd.

"Breakfast, Jimmy," Mama called into the living room. She plunked a heaping platter of fish and scrambled eggs down onto the table. "Help your-selves, everyone," she said, then sighed, looking out the window.

"This will do for me," Daddy said, sitting in front of the platter. "What are the rest of you hav-ing for breakfast?"

Mama didn't laugh at Daddy's daily joke, just tipped a lopsided smile. "It's so beautiful here. Don't you just want to freeze this moment forever?"

Daddy's smile went all askew. "Eat," he told Mama. "We should get on the road to Dexter."

Grampy stayed smoking in the living room, making his true feelings as unmistakable as a fingerprint. He didn't give a hoot about us. And Rebecca and I were stuck alone with him on the best weekend of the summer!

Monday seemed a mountain and an ocean away.

———

I have this idea that would make me a millionaire, if I could just figure out how to do it. The world needs an invention to stop tears from sliding out when you least want them. I could have really used this invention the time Buddy Loring put the jockstrap in my cleats. I needed it when our station wagon started down The Road. Rebecca waved until the dust trail died down, long after the car drove out of sight. She had tears in her eyes. I reached for her hand.

Sometimes my sister drives me so crazy, I think I hate her. Once she took all my *Ellery Queen*s and

cut them up into paper dolls. And I'll never for-
give her for using my baseball cap collection as
party favors on her fifth birthday. But that
moment, holding her hand, I felt closer to
Rebecca than to anyone in the world. I didn't try
to stop her from crying. She needed her tears. But
I held mine back. You can't cry about things like
that when you're almost twelve.

Boonied, right on the minute my team back in
Scranton started practicing to get ready for tomorrow's tourney! It was too much. At the thought of
Buddy Loring devouring the backup pitcher's
meatballs, I sprinted to the bunkhouse so Grampy
wouldn't see the tears I couldn't hold back.

<hr/>

Near noon I went into the camp. Grampy's
rocker creaked now and then on the porch, his
pipe tobacco a light apple scent in the air. Rebecca
was doing that easy puzzle on the lobster-trap
table. I sat on the arm of a chair and built a red
house into the picture.

"Hey, this is my puzzle," said Rebecca, taking
the house apart. "Grampy gave it to me."

"What is it, too hard for him?" I laughed.

45

Rebecca prissed her aren't-*you*-dumb face. "This used to be Daddy's puzzle when he was six. Grampy's putting together one with three thousand pieces."

"Three hundred, you mean." Rebecca hasn't had math yet.

Grampy snickered on the porch.

I practically broke the sound barrier, jetting out there. Grampy had his rocker pulled up to a card table layered with puzzle pieces. It was a three-thousand-piecer, all right. The box showed a round picture—a plate of toast, bacon, and two sunny-side-up eggs. Grampy had the plate all framed in and one egg done.

While Grampy's gnarly fingers sorted through white pieces, I petted Charlie's head. Charlie's tail beat double time on the floor.

"Well?" said Grampy, plucking a piece of the second egg white and snapping it into place.

"Well what?"

"Well, help me make some breakfast?" Tee-hee, ha-ha.

I pulled a lawn chair up in front of the buttered toast, thinking I'd have that together before Grampy even got to his yolk. But those pieces all looked alike, tiny, the same shade of golden brown, hardly any weird nooks and crannies. I was lucky to do the easy little pat of butter by the time Grampy finished that yolk.

I threw down a piece of toast that wouldn't cram in anywhere. "I don't feel like doing this anymore."

Grampy looked at his watch and grunted. "Can't hardly expect to cook a big breakfast in three minutes. What's the problem?"

"I know what it is," Rebecca yelled from the living room. "Timmi's mad because she's missing her baseball game tomorrow."

I swirled around to glare at her through the doorway. "What makes you so smart, squirt!"

She came to the door with her nose in the air. "I saw you throwing a baseball to Charlie after Mama and Daddy left. And Charlie can't even catch."

If I weren't so old, I'd have stuck my tongue out at her.

"What position do you play?" said Grampy. "Outfield?"

Grrr! Typical Buddy Loring thinking: Girls don't play baseball, but if someone lets them on

47

the team, they play right field. I spun around to stare Grampy down.

"Pitcher," I said. "*Starting* pitcher."

"Well, I'll *be!*" He leaned forward and stared right back at me. I didn't like the before-the-punch-line sparkle in his eyes. "You know," he said, "I think we can find you a baseball game tomorrow."

A boonie ball game. That *was* a joke. I could just imagine pitching to Grampy and having to chase the fastballs he missed.

"The young people always have a big baseball game at the Fourth of July picnic in Portage. We'll go so you can play. I have a meeting out there in the morning anyways." Grampy nodded, pleased with himself.

"That's not the same." Did he actually think a hick-town game could take the place of the Independence Tourney?

"Tomorrow's anothuh day, Timothea," Grampy said, and leaned over his breakfast plate.

"*Timmi,*" I said.

"Hm?" He looked up at me.

"Why don't you call me Timmi?"

"Timothea honors your grandmothuh," Grampy said.

"Well, if that's why, I'll be Timothea to you. But"—I glared at Rebecca—"it better not catch on."

Grampy gazed off across the water, his eyes sad. The wind was whipping the lake into white-caps. Motorboats raced around, pitching huge waves against the shore. One red boat with a sharp point and two motors pulled a water-skier right past Grampy's dock. The two men on the boat stood up, whooping and hollering and holding up brown bottles.

"Do you know them, Grampy?" asked Rebecca.

Grampy jolted to his feet and shook his fist toward the boat. "I can't see their faces, but I nevuh seen their boat before. Damned drunken idiots!" he yelled, his face a harsh red. Spit flew from his lips and gleamed on his beard. I'd never seen anyone so angry. Now I knew who Daddy got his "Evils of Alcohol" ideas from.

Rebecca scurried to nestle against me.

"Pardon my French," said Grampy. "But I'm sick of rascals coming here every Fourth of July holiday."

"Aw, Grampy. They're just having a good time," I said.

"Look at them, Timothea! Pollutin' the lake with their racket. There. Heah the poor loons?"

The air rang with an opera of loon shrieks. Big deal. The loons screamed like that when Dale did his impression, and Grampy hadn't shaken any fist at him.

"Those rascals bring their fancy rented boats from who-knows-where and make the rest of us miserable. Go out on the lake with them around, and you're putting your life in their boozed-up hands. What if you girls had been swimming just now? That skier could have sliced right through you."

"Ew, gross," I said.

Grampy, his face pale, slumped back against the wall as the boat grew tiny in the distance. Then he shuffled to the door. "I think I'll lie down for a while. You kids stay out of the watuh. Right?"

I nodded, a little scared. But not because of the boaters. I didn't want to make him mad, a man who could get that angry.

It wasn't long before the green canoe glided up to shore. Dale Chute jogged (joggled, more like) up to the porch and said, "Can't stay long. Mumma sent me over with these." He held out a bagful of pea pods, moist and bright green. I popped a pod open and sucked the sweet tiny peas out.

"You'd best put them in the fridge before your grampy catches you. 'No eating the dinnuh before dinnuh'—that's his rule," said Dale.

"So I've discovered," I said, pinching open another pod. "He's asleep. Want to help me put this puzzle together?"

Dale licked his lips at the breakfast plate. "It sure beats what I've been doing. Fourth of July dinnuh at The Island is fresh garden peas and baby potatuhs in cream, then strawberry short-cake for dessert. My back's killing me. And look." Dale held out his green-stained fingers.

He sat down in Grampy's chair and snapped in some toast pieces as if he was planting seeds.

I whistled. "Tell me this isn't the first time you've worked this puzzle."

"It isn't," he said. "I gave it to Jimmy when he was in the hospital last month, and we put it togethuh togethuh."

"In the hospital?"

"You didn't know?"

No, Dale, I'm just his granddaughter. You're his old buddy old pal. Why were my eyes getting hot and my throat closing in? Didn't I already know Grampy didn't really want me in his life? But I couldn't admit that to Dale.

"No, Mr. Green Thumbs. I mean, did you put the puzzle together in the hospital—on one of those little bed tables?"

He laughed. "I get it. No, we took it to the lounge. He wasn't stuck in bed. He said he was just there for tests. You know, checking out all the plumbing and wiring. 'Typical old man stuff,' he called it."

Maybe that was why Grampy hadn't told his own family. I could just hear him: "Typical tests, nothing to get worked up ovuh." Or maybe he did tell Daddy, and Daddy didn't tell me. Like son, like father.

"Well," said Dale, "now I gotta go back and turn my finguhs red. Strawberries. I could do it tomorrow, but I want to go out to Portage for the big picnic."

After he left, I kept at the puzzle by myself for hours while Rebecca nagged me to help her find four-leaf clovers, build a hideout in the woods next to camp, and come watch a spider spin a web. I was finishing the last slice of bacon when Grampy coughed his way onto the porch and stood over me.

"Well, there," he said, keeping a straight face. "If the sight of all this food don't make me hungry! Think I'll throw togethuh some suppuh." Then he ambled off the porch.

I could have pulverized that man. A whole afternoon I stuck with his puzzle, and he didn't give me so much as a "good job." If he had, I would have told him Dale helped.

We had Grampy's barbecued chicken and potato salad—which I hate to admit I loved—and then went onto the porch to wait for sunset. Rebecca snuggled with me on the swing. "Tell us a scary story, Grampy," she said.

"Well, I don't remembuh no scary *made-up* stories, but I know a true story." Grampy was talking around the empty pipe that dangled from the corner of his mouth. He thoughtfully rubbed his bush of a beard before going on. "But you don't want to hear about that. It's too scary."

"Don't worry," I said. He obviously had scary and boring confused.

"You want to hear about old Chief Hackwithax?"

"Yeah, we do, we do," Rebecca begged.

"All right. But I warned you."

Rebecca grabbed my hand, the chicken.

"Way back before white folks found Fish Lake, the Abnaki tribe lived here."

"Oblunkys?" Rebecca said. "That sounds funny."

"Ab-*nah*-kee. The tribe lived throughout Maine. Their greatest chief was Hackwithax, and he lived t'this side of the lake."

"Hackwax is a weird name," said Rebecca.

As if we really needed her slowing the story down. "So, what happened?" I asked, pushing him on.

"One day Hackwithax—no, I can't tell you. It's too scary. You'll be afraid to sleep in the bunkhouse tonight if you hear the story of Chief Hackwithax. He didn't get his name for nothing, you know."

"Tell us!" squealed Rebecca.

"Yeah!" I said. And hurry up.

"No, I'd bettuh tell you a different story."

We couldn't talk him out of it. He went on and on about Paul Bunyan, the giant logger who single-handedly chopped down the trees to make the city of Bangor. Except Grampy knew something nobody else did: It was really Grampy's grandfather's grandfather, James "Jimbo" Lafler, who did all the work. See, Jimbo was supposedly best friends with Paul Bunyan, but they had this falling out when ol' Paul started taking credit for all the things Grampy's grandfather's grandfather supposedly did.

Bull-oney. And I had to live through two weeks of this.

5

What a dumb sense of humor. Grampy actually thought the way he woke me up the next morning was hilarious. Lucky he didn't give himself a coronary doing it, too—holding Charlie up to lick my face. Talk about disgusting. Dog kisses are gross enough when you can see them coming. I felt grouchier than Lydia Smart did the time Buddy Loring made her quit swimming classes. No matter how smooth she shaved her underarms, Buddy kept saying Lydia had five-o'clock shadow.

After breakfast Rebecca and I squeezed into the passenger seat of Grampy's Jeep to go to Portage for the boonie ball game I wasn't going to play in. I couldn't wait to get there, though, and find Dale. We could swim, call loons, talk about

Grampy. Maybe Rebecca would meet some little kids to play with.

Around the bend from camp, the road was flooded—and not a drop of rain had fallen. Water was spilling over from a pool alongside the road.

"Lookaheah, kids!" said Grampy. "The beavuhs are working on their dam." We stopped to watch a fat beaver chewing on a tree.

"That water's pretty deep," I said. "Can we get through?"

In answer, Grampy shifted gears and barged through the beavers' stick-and-mud curb damming the water on the road.

"Wow." I turned around to watch water flow out of our tire tracks.

"Wow, ayuh. We can knock it down every morning, and the beavuhs will rebuild it by afternoon. If the papuh company was smart, they'd ship them beavuhs upcountry before that pond lets loose and washes out the road something awful."

"Doesn't the paper company own this road and all the forest for miles around?" I asked, remembering the tour-guide talk Daddy had given us on our way up The Road.

"Ayuh," Grampy said, nodding. "And Fish Lake, too."

That surprised me. "You can have a camp on a lake somebody else owns?"

"Can and do—with a ninety-nine–year lease on the land."

"What's that?" asked Rebecca, clinging to the dashboard while the Jeep took to the air after a hulk of a bump.

"The lease gives me the right to stay there, like rent."

"Will you have to move out when the ninety-nine years are over?" The freckles met on Rebecca's scrunched nose.

Grampy looked at her out of the corner of his eye. "The lease can be renewed, deah—not that it will concern me then. A man's lease on life ain't renewable."

"What does that mean?"

Rebecca! I couldn't believe she had no idea. "Grampy will be dead by then," I whispered in her ear.

"Oh." Her eyes went glassy. I put my arm around her and stroked her hair like Mama does to dry up the tears.

We passed the Cow Path gate—Grampy called it the paper-company checkpoint—and turned onto Portage Road. Soon we came across something like civilization. On the right were a playground and the boonie ballpark. The smooth green infield just about made my mouth water. I had to look away. Off to the left, a long, sandy beach opened up a lake that stretched away to the sky. PORTAGE LAKE PUBLIC BEACH, the sign said.

Grampy had his meeting, so he left us off at the beach house. "I'll be back in a little while to watch you pitch, Timothea," he said.

Right.

After Rebecca and I changed into swimsuits, I called, "Last one in's a rotten egg!" and hung back to watch her run her chubby little legs off. She lunged into the water, then turned and yelled, "Na-na-na, Timmi, you're a rotten egg!"

"Heya, Rotten Egg," someone called from the water. "C'mon in, the watuh's great!" Dale's carrot top was bobbing in the waves.

I sprinted down the dock to dive in and came up sputtering. A degree colder, and that water would have been ice.

"Hey, Dale," I said as soon as my lips limbered up, "you told me this water was warm."

"Said *great*, Chicken Skin." He ducked underwater and came back up in the middle of a giant inner tube. I joined him, and we kicked out toward the beach buoys.

"Bet this is the only double-motored inner tube in Maine," I said.

"Like the speedboat on the lake yestuhday. Zoom!" Dale gurgled like a motor.

"You liked that boat, huh?"

"The boat, neat. The guys, dumb jerks," he said between gurgles.

"You call having a little fun being a dumb jerk?"

Dale stopped gurgling. "Guys like that have fun making trouble. They drink and race and yell and don't care one bit about the lake or the people living there."

"That's kind of what Grampy said."

"He's a pretty good guy, your grampy. Lord, he loves Fish Lake."

Too bad he didn't feel the same way about granddaughters, I thought. I tipped my head back, looking toward the sun, and jammed my eyelids shut. Warmth exploded, orange and purple. "Can't you get those dumb-jerk rascals off your lake?"

"No, it's the papuh company's lake—"

"I know, but you live there," I cut in.

"—and *they* let the campers past the checkpoint! All summuh long, people camp on Fish Lake. The only time things get rowdy is the Fourth of July. Mumma says it must be the same bunch of guys every year."

"So, complain to the paper company," I was telling Dale when *crack,* a bat hit a ball and shouting followed. The world's best sound.

"Let's watch the game," said Dale, pushing toward shore. "We're playing Presque Isle. Best team in The County."

That's how he said it—The County—like The Road and The Island. As if I should be impressed! But I decided to go anyway, for a good laugh. I grabbed Rebecca's hand and pulled her along.

The sight of that sloping pitcher's mound and those fresh white baselines sent a thrill through me. Timmi, I reminded myself, this is just boonie baseball. As we joined Grampy in the crowded home stands, the Portage shortstop dug a sizzling ground ball out of the dust. His throw beat the runner to second, and the second baseman zinged the ball to first for a double play. The crowd cheered.

Big deal. If the shortstop couldn't field, nobody could.

"Two outs," said Dale, reading the scoreboard, "and we're winning, zero to nothing."

Grampy laughed. That figured. " 'Bout time you got heah," he said. "Get dressed, Timothea, and check in with the coach."

I shook my head. "Shucks. Wouldn't you know, I left my clothes in the changing house?"

Oh, to have a starship transporter to beam me down to Scranton. I'd have traded anything—even my complete *Ellery Queen* collection. First I'd stop by home to get my cleats and uniform, and then—

Nah. There was no use wishing for a miracle, so I hoped something lively would happen in Portage instead. Maybe a couple outfielders would collide, or an infielder would let the ball roll between his feet, or the second baseman would throw the ball over the first baseman's head.

A scream sliced the air and everyone jumped up. With all the noise, I couldn't make out what anyone said. I hopped up and down on the bleacher to see what was going on. The Portage infielders were bunched around the pitcher, helping him limp off the field. That wasn't what I'd had in mind.

"Oh, no! Not our only pitcher," Dale said. "Now it'll be dark before we even get up to bat."

Sure enough, the new pitcher warmed up by walking seven batters. I may have come for laughs, but this guy was too lousy to be funny. When the number four went up on the scoreboard, people started leaving the stands. At the top of the first, that's bad.

The Portage coach turned around and threw his arms up in the air. "Can *anyone* heah throw a ball ovuh the plate? Even a *slow*ball!"

Rebecca sprang up, pointed to me, and shouted, "My sister is the best pitcher in the whole world!"

I put my hands in front of my face and shook my head. "Shut your trap, squirt."

The coach glanced at me, then smiled at Rebecca. "Sounds like just what we need," he said.

I didn't like the look on the man's face. I'd seen that look on plenty of faces before. It said, "Girl pitcher, huh? Ha-ha-ha. Tell me another one." Something pinches my gut when I see that look.

"If I had my glove, I'd show him," I muttered.

Without a word, Grampy reached into a bag between his feet and pulled out my mitt. He winked as he handed it to me.

"Hey, Timmi, it's gonna *take* the best pitchuh in the world to pull this one off," said Dale, laughing at me.

I didn't appreciate the remark.

Barefoot and in my bathing suit, I ran out on the field to show that coach and Dale Chute I could too put a ball over the plate. Nobody got a chance to yell "She's no pitcher." I pretended the batter was Buddy Loring and sent that first warm-up pitch right down the middle.

It didn't matter that I was playing boonie ball— pitching again felt powerfully good. Like a thunderstorm that wipes out the wet heat of August.

If you think like Dale, we won one to nothing after I started pitching. But Presque Isle had already racked up those runs before I started, so if you think like an umpire, we lost four to one. Our run was an accidental homer at the bottom of the ninth. The guy sucker-swung at a high, outside pitch that even Buddy Loring would have let pass by. That Buddy, he'd try to whomp a potato out of the park if you threw it anywhere near him.

You'd think the Portage team would have been thankful for the rescue, but they didn't exactly carry me off the field with joy. They just said, "Hey, you're pretty good. For a girl." Then they ran off for a swim without inviting me. But they invited Dale. And he went!

For a girl—*grrr*. As I started toward Grampy to complain, three barrel-bellied men wearing KISS THE COOK aprons staggered past me, hauling coolers and charcoal grills out onto the field.

"Hey, girlie, howdja learn to hurl like that?" slurred the guy with the biggest belly. He opened a cooler, cracked open a beer bottle, and swigged. As if he needed another one.

"The same way as the *boyies*," I said. "Practice."

"Practice, huh? Well, you won't be keeping up

with the boys when Mother Nature gets aholt of you."

The other two almost fell down laughing. But they were so drunk they were almost falling down dumping charcoal, too.

"That's enough, Fogg," called Grampy, climbing down from the bleachers with Rebecca.

The guy with the bottle laughed, looking at me. "C'mon, Jimmy. You evuh seen a star pitchuh with full-feathuhed parakeets? There's nothing to her now, but . . ."

The moment I figured out what he meant, my breath left me. People are always saying lousy things about me playing ball, but nobody else has ever made a crack like that.

Grampy put his hand on my shoulder. "*That* was crass, Fogg! You owe my granddaughtuh an apology."

The man's face reddened like a sunburn. "Your granddaughtuh? Oh, cow manuah! I'm sorry, Jimmy. I thought she was just some tourist's kid showing off."

Oh, sure. Then it would be all right to mouth off like that.

"Hey, Jimmy. Why don't you join us?" One of the charcoal dumpers held up a whiskey bottle.

Grampy shook his head. "Don't touch the stuff."

The three men looked at each other and howled with laughter.

"Whatevuh you say, *old granddad,*" Fogg said.

"That's the booze talking, boys." Grampy's face was stiff and red-mad.

"Are those men your friends, Grampy?" whispered Rebecca.

"I used to think so, a long time ago," he whispered back.

Grampy took Rebecca's hand and tipped his head toward the road. "Come on, girls. No sense letting a couple drunks ruin our holiday."

Who needed hot dogs grilled by jerks in KISS THE COOK aprons anyway.

Grampy's face stayed hard as a clamshell all the way home. He didn't say a word, except a couple pardon-my-French ones when we jostled over some road craters, and then he muttered, "I seen a doe run to death on The Road. Them Fogg fools chased aftuh her in a pickup truck till she just keeled over. I'd 'a' liked to wrung those boys' necks."

Now I knew where Daddy got his weird streak. Now I knew where he got a lot of streaks.

Feelings of missing Mama and Daddy whisked around in my stomach, anger mixing in. I felt like yelling down to Dexter how Daddy and Mama ruined the best day of summer by leaving Scranton, leaving camp, leaving Grampy to haul me into Portage.

Parakeets! Even Buddy Loring wasn't that disgusting. What an outhouse of a day this was turning out to be. And it was only half over.

6

*B*ack at camp, Grampy made tuna salad (after assuring Blue Eyes it was dolphin-free) and we had our own picnic on the lawn.

"Grampy, I'm bored," said Rebecca as soon as she swallowed her last bite.

"Bored!"

I thought he'd be like Mama and rattle off a list of things we'd already done to death, but he didn't.

"Follow me," said Grampy, ambling up the path to camp. He went into the living room and lifted the top off the lobster-trap table, careful not to upset Rebecca's completed city. Boxes upon boxes of puzzles were lined up in the trap.

"We'll have us a puzzle-put'n-togethuh contest. First one done wins. Rebecca, you pick out one with a hundred pieces. Timothea, three—no, five hundred. I'll take me a thousand-piecer."

"You, a thousand?" I squinted at him. "Fifteen hundred. And I choose."

He laughed. "You drive a hard bargain. All right. Fifteen hundred it is. One piece at a time."

"I'll take this one," said Rebecca, demolishing her city.

"Ain't you a smarty." Grampy grinned at her and shuffled out onto the porch to break up the breakfast puzzle.

"Cheater, more like," I said.

"Nuh-unh. Grampy said I could pick."

I rolled my eyes and bent over the lobster trap, pulling out landscapes, cities, farms, animals, people, gardens. I decided on a circus with lots of different animals and people I could match against the box picture.

For Grampy I picked an aquarium of marbles— every one as clear as water. Every piece would look alike. I grinned as I handed it to him. Grampy shrilled a got-my-work-cut-out whistle and dumped the marbles out onto the card table.

"No way, Jack," I said. "The puzzle stays in the box until we're all ready to start."

"Oh, ayuh. Fair's fair." He pushed the pieces back into the box while Rebecca and I claimed space on the floor.

"On your mark," said Rebecca, "get set . . . go!"

Puzzle pieces showered out of boxes, and the silent sorting frenzy began. *Turn all the pieces right-side up, collect all the straight edges as you go, keep like colors together. Save a wide-open space to work the puzzle, but the cage pieces can go right in the middle.* A quick glance up—*Grampy's already framed in the aquarium. But edges are always easy. Those marbles will slow him down, oh ayuh. Rebecca's putting together that easy red house first. She'll never win like that. You gotta have a plan.*

While working, I kept watch on Grampy out of the corner of my eye, like keeping tabs when Buddy Loring's on first and aiming to steal second. Finally I was down to the center ring of elephants herded together, and Grampy was closing in the middle gap. All nervous, I started jamming puzzle nubs into any old crook. *Don't lose your cool, Timmi. Don't force it.*

With one last elephant's-tail piece to go, I glanced up, expecting Grampy to be sitting there done, just a-gloating like Buddy when he beats my throw back to first. But the aquarium still had a gap, and Grampy was sound asleep in his rocker, his unlit pipe dangling loosely from his lips.

"Sheesh." I threw the elephant's tail down. Sure, I wanted to win, but not like that. A contest to stop boredom, and Grampy fell asleep.

"I wonder why Grampy's so tired all the time?" I whispered to Rebecca. "He hardly does a thing all day except sit smoking and doing puzzles."

"Babies don't do anything all day, either, and they take naps every afternoon," said Rebecca.

Now that was a thought—an old man sleeping like a baby.

Lying on my stomach and resting my head on my hand, I stared at Grampy's face. Lunch crumbs clung to the whiskers around his lips. His mouth fell open. The deep wrinkles under his eyes stretched smooth and the pipe tumbled onto his lap. His head bobbed slightly with each grumbly breath, and a piece of wiry gray hair stuck out at the top. It seemed to wave at me.

I can't imagine being that old. Me, I'm never going to look older than twenty. By the time I'm that old, someone will figure out a way to make people live forever. Maybe someone will even find that fountain of youth the social studies teacher told us about. They can make Coke and Pepsi out of the water, and everyone will stay young. I might turn seventy like Grampy, but I'll never look like him.

Didn't I jump right then! Loud shots boomed across the lake. Rebecca dived on top of me, screaming. Grampy snorted awake.

"Hush up, Jimbo!" he cried hoarsely. He shuddered before he opened his eyes. "Oh!" he said. "It's you."

More booms echoed, and the air vibrated. "Firecrackers," I said, prying my sister off me. "People shoot them off every Fourth of July in Scranton." I got up and looked across the lake.

"Against the law," said Rebecca, sounding just like Mama the year I wanted to get some firecrackers.

Grampy pulled himself up and stood looking out the window, rubbing his temples. "Those wisecracking rascals are up to their Fourth of July jackassery again."

Rebecca giggled at the naughty-sounding word.

The firecracking jackassery sounded like fun to me. "Aw, Grampy. What do you want them to do for fun around here? Puzzle contests?" I bent over to click the elephant's tail into place.

"Timmi beat Grampy, Timmi beat Grampy," taunted Rebecca.

Grampy took a chesty breath and let it out slow. "I told Jimbo the city would spoil you. You know the problem with the world today? Noise. Nobody knows how to enjoy just being alive, quietlike." Grampy tipped his head at me, an idea sparkling in his eyes.

"What do you think our ancestuhs used to do for fun, gals? Before televisions, radios, stereos, and malls of people all talking to once?"

"Well," said Rebecca, all serious, "one guy chopped down the trees to make Bangor, but it wasn't much fun having Paul Bunyan get all the credit, I bet."

Grampy tee-heed as he unhooked three orange life preservers from the porch wall. "Come on, you two. I'm going to show you some real fun. We're going rowing."

"Yay!" cried Rebecca. "What's rowing?"

"C'mon," I said. "You'll see." As I ran to the dinghy, a thrill swelled in my stomach. I'd skim across the water like Dale! I jumped in and rocked the boat, getting the feel.

"Hold it, Timothea," Grampy said, pointing at me. "That boat—" A hacking cough stopped him. You'd think he would quit all that smoking. "That boat ain't no toy. Heah. Put this on." He tossed a life preserver at me.

Grimacing, I strapped it on. It was so thick and bulky that I could hardly move. Did he think I didn't know how to swim? "Dale Chute doesn't wear one of these dumb things," I said.

"He should. Even the best of us can have an accident."

The best of *us*? That would include Grampy. I had to giggle, thinking of him doing the doggy paddle.

"You, too, Rebecca," Grampy said, wrapping her in orange. I couldn't see much of her under the adult-sized vest—only a blond head at the top and fat legs at the bottom.

As Grampy vested himself, Rebecca hopped into the dinghy and sat in the tip. I sat in the middle, back to her, and put the oars in the locks. Grampy wobbled one foot into the dinghy and lurched into the stern, the motor end, facing me. I shoved the right paddle into the water and pulled back. The dinghy thwacked the dock.

"A little impatient, now, aren't we," Grampy said, panting like a hot dog. "Give me a second to catch my breath, and I'll explain how to get somewhere in this rig."

"Backseat paddler," I muttered under the firecracker noise.

Grampy told Rebecca how to unlash the front rope. He freed his end, and I pushed off from the dock. The first time I dipped the oars, the dinghy circled around toward shore.

"Timothea, you're paddling too hard on the left," said Grampy. "You ain't trying to bash a baseball with that oar."

Finally I managed to row without turning circles. We zigzagged beyond the cove, leaving the camp out of sight. Grampy pointed to a boulder Daddy used to call Elephant Rock and a driftwood heap where he used to hunt bullfrogs. They could have been the Statue of Liberty and

Niagara Falls, the way Grampy bubbled about them.

"Seeing where Jimbo used to play reminds me of a story," said Grampy. Was there anything that didn't?

"When your fathuh was about the age of Blue Eyes," he started, "he and I went frogging every Saturday. Grammy used to cook the legs, and—"

Rebecca and I screamed, "*Yuck*," agreeing for once.

"Oh, they're delicious—like chicken, only bettuh. You girls catch me some nice big frogs, and I'll cook 'em for you."

"Icky, icky, icky!" squealed Rebecca. She'd wheezed before when an ant crawled across her ceiling. Touching a frog would probably give her an asthma attack. Besides, she wouldn't eat any creature she'd actually met. Just finding out hamburger comes from cows made her throw out an entire Happy Meal.

"Rebecca's sort of allergic to frogs," I said. "Maybe when Daddy gets back."

So, then Grampy told us about this amazing bullfrog Daddy supposedly caught. It had such a tough hide that no knife could skin it. Grampy even tried an ax, he said. Couldn't knock that frog out, the hide was so tough. So Daddy had to let the frog go, and for all Grampy knew, it still lived under a big rotten log in the driftwood heap.

Right, Grampy.

By the time we drifted back to camp, the heat had wafted out of the day, but not out of me. I was hot and tired from rowing, so I jumped into the lake, shorts and T-shirt and all.

"Feels late," said Grampy, checking his watch. "Well, Jiminy Jehoshafat, it'll be dark soon! I'll hustle us up some eats."

At least he didn't say *ets*.

The firecrackers kept popping as Grampy grilled ham steaks and steamed the tiny peas from Mrs. Chute's garden. Swimming in cream, those peas tasted better than the sweet watermelon we had for dessert.

After dinner, sitting on the porch, we saw smoke twisting up from the center of Blueberry Island. It looked like white ribbon curling against gray wrapping paper. Off in the distance, the mountains were wrapped in pink and purple, with the sun trimming them like a fat red bow. I had to sigh.

"Those rascals are on Blueberry. They'll be burning down the island with big camp fires like that," said Grampy. "Well, it's been a long day. Let's turn in. We can get up early and go fish for our breakfast."

I looked forward to that. I'd never caught my own breakfast before, unless you count catching the bagel that flew out of the toaster one time.

In the night, a thundering noise jolted me awake. Rebecca lay whimpering and wheezing in the bottom bunk. She's afraid of lightning, but I think it's pretty.

The noise and light didn't come from a storm. "Tell your lungs it's okay to breathe now," I told Rebecca. "It's just fireworks."

"Like at the park last year?" She puffed on her inhaler.

"Yeah, like that. Want to come up here and watch?"

Rebecca scrambled up the ladder and pressed her nose against the window. The fireworks flew into the air with a whistle, splattered into streams of color, and then echoed like a machine gun. I wished they wouldn't stop, but they did, and Rebecca went back to her bunk.

Grampy was probably hyperventilating from shaking his fist at this jackassery. What a great word. *Bug off, Buddy, and quit the jackassery.*

_7

Charlie licked me awake before the sun rose the next morning.

I rolled over.

Grampy called me "slugabed" and pitched my covers back. Air chilled the drowsiness right out of me. I sprang off the bed and scooted into some sweats.

Grampy made me dig the worms because he was too old, Rebecca was too young, and I was just right. I felt like the baby bear in "Goldilocks."

We got into the dinghy and chugged to the middle of the lake, where Grampy said the Godzilla trout hung out in deep, cold pools near the bottom. Water stretched away and away to the hazy fringe of woods and mountains.

I hooked a squiggly worm and looked at

Grampy. "Did you see those fireworks last night?"

"Couldn't miss 'em, Timothea, coming from Blueberry Island. Might as well have a display right in our own living room."

I cast my line and reeled it quickly in. "I know fireworks are illegal and dangerous, but they sure were pretty." I had to stop reeling to slap a fat mosquito that was snacking on my hand.

"Most of us have bettuh things to do at midnight than to listen to jackanapes disturbing the peace," Grampy said.

Jackanapes. Where did he get his excellent words!

Grampy flicked his pole. The line sailed a perfect arc. The bait plunked softly into the water. Circles surrounded the plastic orange bob like the rings of Saturn. "Those dang fools could have blown themselves up."

I watched the rings spread to nothingness around Grampy's bob, then recast my line.

"Timothea, let the bait sink a bit before reeling in. We ain't fly-fishing! Trout are used to worms that take their time getting places. Reel your line slooowly."

Right, I thought, those trout are used to worms that get places the way Grampy tells stories.

"Ick," Rebecca said, holding the slimy worm can in my face. "Will you bait my hook?"

"I love the way you say *please*," I said, but I grabbed the can. "You shouldn't be let within ten feet of a fishing pole until you can worm your own hook, or hook your own worm. Here."

I returned to my own fishing. Nobody said anything for a while. Finally my bob dunked underwater, dragging my rod into an arc, and the boat tipped sideways. "Hey, I got something!"

"Looks like a good 'un," Grampy said. "Calm yourself. Reel in firmly, but with a light touch. And for God's sake, if he fights, give him some line. These trout don't have no dentists to cap their teeth."

"Whoopee ding," I said, reeling. "Fish don't need dentists."

Grampy *tsk*ed. "You yank on that line too hard, and the hook will rip through the trout's mouth. Broken teeth can cause a fish to starve to death. No sport in that."

"Oh." Carefully, I reeled and reeled, let some line go when the fish tugged, reeled, and reeled some more. At last a dark shadow appeared just under the surface a few feet away. In a sudden splash, the trout soared out of the water. Its sides sparkled, gray with pale spots of color, and its belly gleamed pure white. That trout had to be two feet long.

Rebecca dived for the big net in the bottom of the dinghy. The fish shot back underwater, and the line went slack. My fishing rod straightened. I reeled in quickly, but nothing came up at the end of the line. No trout. No worm. No hook.

"Booger," said Rebecca, putting the net back down.

"You can say that again," I said, staring at the naked line. But I didn't really see it. I saw that fish—beautiful as a rainbow.

"Boog*uh*!" said Rebecca.

Grampy was grinning. "Well, Timothea, welcome to the world of the one that got away. The same thing happened to me once. Why, that fish was ten feet long if it was an inch. Jimbo and I was up Houlton way, oh, about thirty years back, when—"

"Bloody mosquitoes!" I slapped another bug on

my arm. During the battle with the fish, they had come to Timmi's Mosquitaurant for breakfast, lunch, and dinner.

Grampy frowned at me and put down his pole. "That's mad talk I'm hearing. Guess we've had us enough fishing for one day." He started the motor with one quick yank of the cord. The dinghy chugged slowly toward the distant brown speck that was Grampy's camp.

"Say, Timothea, want to learn to drive the boat?"

I didn't say anything, thinking about that fish.

"I do, I do!" piped Rebecca. Her voice bounced back at us from all sides: "IdooIdooIIdoodoo."

I glared at her and moved to sit with Grampy in the stern. He cut the motor. The dinghy slowed and drifted with the waves.

"All right, Timothea. If the motor ain't been started for a while, you got to prime it by pulling out the chuck."

"The *chuck*?" Rebecca and I chimed in.

Grampy laughed and pointed to a black knob.

"Oh!" I said, remembering the knobs on our lawn mower. "The *choke*."

"But you don't got to put the chuck to the

motor today, since she's already warmed up," said Grampy.

I grabbed the cord handle.

"Hold it there!" Grampy put a hand on my arm. "You got to learn to steer first, or we'll end up in Timbuktu."

"I guess if I can strike out the Presque Isle Pros, I can steer a stupid boat," I told him.

Grampy pointed to the lever at the side of the motor and explained how it controlled the direction of the boat. He also made sure I chugged along *slooowly*.

On the way back to camp, I steered close to Blueberry Island, where the red boat with a sharp point and two motors rocked in a tiny cove. You could look through the trees and see the water on the other side. Three green pup tents were pitched in the middle of the island.

"Trespassuhs," Grampy yelled in their direction. "Them tomfools oughta be plunked with a big fine and sleep off their party mood in the hoosegow—"

"That means jail, Rebecca," I cut in, but Grampy was still talking. The more he talked, the redder his face got.

"—and the powers that be at the papuh company oughta be strung up by their toenails for looking the other way."

It huffs me up, people running off their mouths about stuff instead of *doing* something. And when I'm huffed up, the words just gush out. "Grampy, we're not the ones you should be complaining to."

I winced when Grampy snapped around to look at me. He'd probably call that "back talk" and land the boat on Blueberry to cut him a switch. But he smiled that lopsided smile of Daddy's and said, "You know, Timothea, you got yourself a point."

I was so hungry when we got back, cornflakes tasted great. A few minutes later, Dale canoed over with a message: His mother wanted us to come to dinner that night. I was glad to see someone, anyone, even one who'd abandoned me at the ball field. I begged him to stay and play Clue, but he had to hurry back to The Island and weed The Beets.

As Dale paddled homeward, I had an idea. I ran to untie the dinghy. "See you later," I called to Grampy, who was rocking on the porch.

Rebecca raced out of the camp. "I wanna go, too!"

"No you don't. I'm going *bullfrogging*," I white-lied.

"Timothea, take your sister with you," Grampy called, "if she's brave enough to go, with you rowing."

"Yeah," Rebecca piped.

"No using the motor until you've had more lessons, got it?" he added.

"Yeah," I groaned.

"Run up heah, Blue Eyes, and get some life pre-servers," Grampy went on. "And stay close to shore, Timothea!" he hollered. "The water can get rough before you know it!"

Rowing is sort of like learning a new pitch—you have to get the feel of it. With each stroke, I felt more and more in control. Nothing in the world is quite like rowing. Breeze rushing against you, water spraying you, sun beating down.

Alongside the driftwood heap I sprang my idea. "Rebecca, want to go help Dale weed the garden?"

"Grampy said not to go away from shore. Dale always goes across the lake. He lives a zillion trillion miles away."

I crossed my fingers. "Bah, Grampy won't mind if we go out deeper, now that I'm so good at rowing."

"No!"

I gave up for a while and paddled on silently, still itching to explore The Island. Then I noticed Blueberry jutting out of the water just a quarter of a mile away.

"Rebecca?" I was so sweet, I disgusted myself. "Want to go look at Blueberry Island? It's only a minute away."

She tipped her head sideways, thinking.

"A minute isn't very far away from shore," I said. "We could see what Grampy's rascals look like."

More silent thinking, then, "Okay. We could tell them to stop disturbing the peace. Then Grampy wouldn't get a red face and spit on his beard." That Rebecca. She was starting to like the old man.

I wasn't about to tell a bunch of full-grown

jackanapes to cut out the jackassery, but Rebecca didn't need to know that. We'd just row near enough for a little innocent spying.

Getting to Blueberry took longer than I'd expected. The deeper the water, the rougher the waves got. Thank goodness the red boat was gone. My sore arms needed rest. I pulled the dinghy onto the pebbly beach and sloughed off that straitjacket of a life preserver.

"Boy, was that a long minute!" Rebecca said as she unbuckled her vest.

"You'd better leave that on in case we need to make a quick getaway," I told her.

She slitted her eyes—her stubborn look. "Only if you do."

Living with Rebecca, you learn when not to argue. I strapped the vest back on.

The double-motored boat wasn't anywhere in sight. We had some time to look around. Then it hit me: We might find some jackassery evidence to take to the paper company—maybe some burnt-out firecrackers or packages that the fireworks came in.

"Come on," I said. "Let's explore."

The place was a giant rock covered with enough dirt to grow a blanket of brush and a stand of pines and maples. The rascals' three tents took up most of the center clearing.

"Look where the fire was," said Rebecca, pointing between the tents to a circle of stones. "Yuck. It stinks."

Burnt-smelling smoke feathers rose from a charred log at the edge of the fireplace, but the mound of ashes inside looked wet. Good—the rascals had enough wits to douse their fire.

Outside the clearing, between some bushes, I spied a mound of moist dirt. At first I thought someone had been digging for worms. Then the odor drifted our way.

"Ooh, it smells like the bathroom after Daddy reads the morning paper in there." Rebecca pinched her nose.

"Jiminy Jehoshafat, they fergut to flush," I said. We laughed and laughed.

Beyond that was another dirt pile, which didn't stink. It bulged up like someone sleeping under a quilt. "Something's buried in there," I said.

"Something big," said Rebecca.

"A body, maybe." I stood over it and stared down.

"Blowed up by firecrackers."

I was in so much awe, imagining body pieces packed underground, that I didn't even correct Rebecca's lousy English.

Rebecca scooched to pull something out of the dirt, then stood. "Why would they bury a candy wrapper with the body?"

"Let's find out." I toed some dirt away from the mound. A piece of metal shone under a sunbeam that filtered through the trees. I hadn't noticed before how creepy the treetops were, a shadowy roof of leaves swaying over us.

Rebecca reached for the metal.

"Don't touch that!" I shrieked. What if the body hadn't been firecrackered to death? What if the demise wasn't accidental? "It might be the murder weapon!"

She jumped back and covered her mouth. "What are we going to do?" asked Rebecca in a small voice.

What would Sherlock Holmes do? "Let's get Grampy. No, let's dig this up. It would be pretty embarrassing if Grampy came here and there wasn't any body. But it would be pretty gross to dig one up. Buddy Loring would do it. Oh, I don't know!"

Rebecca took a deep breath. "If somebody might be buried here, we should find out."

She pushed some dirt away and uncovered a can. The dirt inside it was orange-red. I was horrified. "Blood," I whispered, pointing.

"Blood?"

I nodded. That can probably had a sharp, sawed-off bottom, an improvised murder weapon.

Rebecca grimaced as she pried the can from the dirt and held it out, pinched between two fingers. "Look, those Jacks disguised the murder weapon as a giant tomato-soup can."

I snatched it away from her. The soggy, dirt-caked label flapped from yellow glue dots. I ripped the paper off and stomped it into the dirt.

"Cripes, there's no body buried here. Just trash. The jackanapassery slobs!" Actually I was relieved—imagining finding a dead body is fun, but finding one wouldn't be.

I placed the can upside down on the mound and jumped on it. My sneakers, still wet from shoring the dinghy, sounded squishy.

Then we heard the motorboat.

8

*T*he motor revved and then stopped, revved and then stopped, coming toward the island. Weird, yes, but I wasn't going to stand around figuring out what was wrong. Rebecca and I bolted to the dinghy and rowed away.

The motor was the glossy red boat, all right. Chasing a moose across the lake! The boat would lag back, then speed toward the moose, which was frantic to stay ahead of that boat—neck straining to keep nose above water, antlers bobbing through the waves. The three men's laughter rang over the water.

"Cripes. That makes me sick," I said.

Rebecca was crying. "How can people scare a poor animal like that?"

The boat revved up to the moose's backside again, and I recognized the men—those jerks who'd had Kiss the Cook aprons on over their *parakeets* after the Portage ball game. Didn't it figure.

"We have to do something to stop them!" Rebecca snatched her inhaler from her sock and took a puff. Getting upset sets her to wheezing lickety-split.

"Let's stay levelheaded, Rebecca," I said, thinking of Daddy. "Those guys have been drinking. I'm scared of them."

"So's that moose," said Rebecca, "only it can't say so." And she stood right up in the dinghy to yell, "Hey, you Jacks, stop it!"

With my sister being brave like that, I couldn't just sit there. I stood up, too, and yelled along with her. "Stop it! Stop it! Stop it!"

Our shouting and the men's laughing ricocheted from all directions, and I didn't hear Grampy's boat approaching until it roared alongside us. Grampy didn't stop, just waved for us to sit down. We did when the wake of his boat set the dinghy to rocking.

Grampy circled wide around the moose and idled near the red boat. "You sons o' horses want to chase something, go play football," he hollered. "Let the moose be."

You tell 'em, Grampy.

The men cackled.

"Think it's funny?" Grampy must have had a red face then. "You'll think it's funny camping out in jail. Because if you don't get your behinds off this lake today, I'm reporting you!"

"Oh yeah, Jimmy?" yelled one of the guys. "It's your word against ours, old man. You can't prove *nothing.*"

Grampy didn't answer back. He set off to guard the moose, which had swum past us, headed toward the driftwood heap. The red boat zoomed to the Blueberry Island cove. I rowed to camp. Grampy got there right after us, muttering to himself, the veins standing out on his neck. Rebecca and I tied up the boat.

All quavery, Grampy could hardly lift his leg onto the dock. "Here, let me help," I said, and reached out so he could hoist himself up on my arm.

"Boy, Grampy," I said on the path to camp, "if you hadn't gone out there when you did, what would have happened to that moose?"

Frowning, he shook his head. "Might have run out of energy and drowned. Could have had a heart attack, hyperventilated, just been plumb scared to death. Heck, the poor beast might still die because of them Fogg fools. . . . I should have known it was them rabble rousuhs out to Blueberry. Last summer, I heard they rented themselves a fancy boat and got Portage Lake all riled up. Guess they didn't think nobody on Fish Lake would give a hoot."

"I'm glad you're my grampy," Rebecca said, squeezing his thigh the way she does to Daddy when he gets home from work.

"Why, thank you!" said Grampy, a smile tripping across his face. "Jiminy, you're good girls." He stopped and crossed his arms, the smile sliding away. "But that don't mean you won't be punished for leaving the shoreline!"

I'd almost forgotten about that. A shiver ran through my scalp as my thoughts jumped to Grampy's temper, the switch thing, spare the rod.

I stepped back and covered my tush without even thinking about it.

Grampy's punishment surprised me, though. "No using the dinghy for three days," he proclaimed as if he was exiling us from the kingdom.

"That it?" I asked, relieved.

"Ain't it enough?" He looked truly puzzled.

After lunch, Grampy read magazines in his rocker. Rebecca sat on the floor cutting gangs of paper dolls out of newspapers. I pulled Grampy's puzzle table up to the porch swing and started a thousand-piecer. It was gorgeous—and hard. Grass and sky with a strip of ocean in between, and off to the side a sailboat cutting across a ball of sun. It was even hard getting the edges together, with the colors so pure. After half an hour, I groaned and got up to stretch my raw rowing muscles.

"You'll do well if you get that puzzle togethuh before your folks get back," said Grampy. "If you get it togethuh at all."

I tried to stare him down for saying that, but he

just kept a straight face. I plunked back down onto the swing.

"I guess prob'ly I'll get this togethuh before the folks get back," I drawled. A perfect Grampy impression, I must say.

Grampy chuckled in that way of his. "Timothea, you're a lot like someone else I used to know." He grinned wickedly, showing a mouthful of even, yellowed teeth. He got up from his chair and wagged a bony finger at me. "Now, you wait heah!" He disappeared into his bedroom, leaving me curious.

Soon Grampy shuffled back, carrying a thick, peeling photo album with yellowed edges sticking out. He gently placed it on top of my puzzle. All the bones in his body must have cracked as he sat beside me on the swing and pulled his legs across each other. He looked like some ancient chief.

"What is all this junk?" I said.

"Junk! This is not junk. This," he said with a grand gesture of his long, skinny arms, "is my life."

"It's a photo album," Rebecca announced.

"Thanks, Queen Ellery," I said.

Grampy leafed through the album. Gray people dressed in old-fashioned clothes stared out from each page. He stopped at the pretty face of a young woman, the very same picture hanging in our hallway back in Scranton.

"That's Grammy," Rebecca and I said together.

Next was a picture of a boy about my age. He was thin and his hair and eyes were dark.

"Hey, look, that's you, Timmi," Rebecca said, gaping.

I elbowed her. "That's a boy, idiot." All I needed was my own sister thinking I was a boy, too, and becoming an informant for the peek-at-Timmi-in-the-bathroom club.

"Besides," I said, "that picture is *old*." The yellow edges curled up, and the boy was made up of little black dots.

"Well, it looks like you," Rebecca insisted.

"Maybe it's Daddy," I said. It looked like Daddy's smile, dimply around the ends, taking over his face.

"That boy is old enough now to be your fathuh's fathuh," said Grampy, prying his legs uncrossed.

Then I knew. Grampy's eyes sat in a hollow of

wrinkled skin, but still they looked the same as the boy's in the picture. "It's you," I said softly. I'd never thought of it before—Grampy being anything but a gruff old man.

"I used to be a firecrackuh like you, Timothea," Grampy said in a faraway voice. "Lord, to be able to do it all over again, knowing what I know now."

He leaned back in the swing and propped his hands behind his neck, elbows out to the sides. "I got so angry when things didn't go my way. Sometimes . . . well, I did things I came to regret. I've finally learned there's things worth getting the fantods about, and things best left alone." When he finally looked at me, his smile had a bittersweet way about it, like Mama's in the bunkhouse when she said Grampy wanted to wrap up his life and put a bow on it.

Grampy had obviously hidden away a headful of Daddy history, too, but with that look on his face, I couldn't ask for his side of the story.

<hr>

It was time to head for the Chutes' place. Rebecca and I unlashed the big boat while Grampy peered off into the gray distance, shielding his eyes with his hands. "Looks like a storm a-brewing," he said.

The wind pulled at our shirtsleeves as we crossed the lake, the waves rising into a white froth like meringue. Rebecca's teeth were chattering. Goose pimples dotted her arms.

"Grampy," I shouted over the roaring motor, "Rebecca needs to stay warm. This cold air's bad for her asthma."

"Ayuh? Well, get the blanket out of the trunk, there."

I dug into the chest beneath the hull and pulled out a plaid blanket.

"It's wool," I said.

"S'pose she's allergic to that?"

I nodded.

Grampy stripped off his flannel shirt and gave it to Rebecca. It fit her like a dress made for a long-armed monkey. Grampy looked pretty comical, too, with his sleeveless V-neck T-shirt. Now he had the goose pimples. I hadn't realized just how scrawny he was until the wind flattened the cotton against his chest and I counted ten of his ribs. I threw the wool blanket at him, and he wore it like a teepee.

At last the boat neared a big chunk of land looming out of the lake. Sprays of water stung my face as we veered toward shore. Dale ran down the dock to catch the boat.

"Some wind, don't you think?" he said. His hair blew to the side like a cockeyed rooster's comb as he led us up a sloped path between rows of dark pines. Dale pointed out the rental cabins huddled among the pine boughs.

"We have a full camp this weekend," he said.

In the center of The Island was a garden the size of an infield. I hit Dale's arm. "You weed that!"

"If I want to eat, I do." He patted that stomach of his. Of course I laughed.

Dale stopped in front of a weather-beaten log cabin and held the door open for us.

His mother hurried toward us, rubbing her hands on her apron. She was a grown-up version of Dale, round and redheaded. "Welcome! Hello, Jimmy. Good to see you." She nodded at Grampy. He grunted a hello.

Dale's mother turned to me. "Timothea! I've been looking forward to meeting you ever since your grampy said you were coming to visit." She squeezed my shoulders and smiled.

I had to wonder what she'd heard. Before a few days ago, what had Grampy known about me to tell?

"Call her Timmi, Mumma, if you want to live," said Dale. "She hates the name Timothea."

Real thoughtful, saying that in front of Grampy. "I don't *hate* it. It just doesn't suit me," I said, glaring at Dale.

"Timmi it is, then. And Rebecca. What a sweetheart!" Dale's mother ran her fingers through Rebecca's hair. "I always wanted Dale to have a little sister just like you."

"He can have *her*," I blurted.

Rebecca stuck her tongue out at me.

While Mrs. Chute was passing plates, Grampy cleared his throat. "Well, the girls and I had an adventure this morning."

"What happened?" asked Dale.

"Rebecca and I went rowing," I started, "and we—"

"Tell them about that poor moose!" Rebecca cut in.

Dale bent toward me across his pork chop. "What poor moose?"

"I was getting to that." I rolled my eyes at Rebecca. Now Dale wasn't going to let me build up my story. I had to plunge right in at the high point.

"Well, you know those guys with the red boat who've been camping out on Blueberry? Today we caught them chasing a moose across the lake. They'd zoom that boat right up to him and laugh while he tried to swim faster."

The Chutes gasped. "I can't believe anyone would do that," said Dale.

"Oh, them Fogg boys from out to Portage done it, all right. I told them to get their hinders off our lake, or else," said Grampy.

"My job depends on people coming to enjoy Fish Lake," said Mrs. Chute, "but times like this I almost wish we could put a dome over it to keep humans out. Just a few careless people seem to spoil every good thing. Torturing an animal like that!"

Grampy nodded. "I agree. And that's why me and the girls are going to file a complaint with the papuh company tomorrow."

I snapped a look at Grampy. "Really? You didn't tell me."

"I just decided this minute. People who love something can't let it be spoiled."

Grampy looked at me weird right then. At first I thought maybe he figured I was spoiled, spoiled by Jimbo, and he was going to put a stop to it. But then he leaned the sweetest smile at me, his eyes a gush of happiness. You couldn't fake a look like that. It caught me like a line drive: Maybe Grampy really did care. Embarrassed, I looked away.

"Those dumb jerks ought to be arrested. Are they still on Blueberry?" asked Dale.

"Good question, Dale," said Grampy. "You kids should ride by there and see. Don't get too close if the boat's still there. And come right back if it starts to rain." He tossed Dale the boat keys.

_9

*T*he red boat and the pup tents were gone. "Come on," I said. "Let's go ashore and dig up some evidence to take to the paper company. Hey!" I laughed. *"Dig up some evidence!"*

"What's so funny?" Dale cut the motor. As we moored in the Blueberry cove, I told him about the garbage grave.

"What do they think Blueberry is, a landfill?" Dale snatched an oar out of the storage area and ran. I raced after him with the other oar. We plunged the oars into the dirt mound, looking for packaging and scraps of burnt-out fire-works.

After a while of digging and heaping garbage, Dale said, "Enough glass heah to keep a recycling centuh busy for a week," and pulled out two more beer bottles.

"Those jackanapes-jerks celebrated enough for a year," I said.

"What's this?" Rebecca held out a dirt-caked, rocket-shaped silver tube with a char-blackened bottom.

I took it and wiped the crud off on my sweats, uncovering a string of red print. "'Warning,'" I read. "'Explosive substance. Handle with extreme caution.'"

"Fireworks!" said Dale. "That one's a dud."

I wagged the rocket at him. "This will prove that those guys were here breaking the law."

Dale grinned at me. "And, in case eyewitnesses ain't enough, this will prove who they were!" He waved a piece of crumpled paper.

I took it and squinted to make out the words, blotchy from the wet earth. It was a receipt from Service Merchandise in Presque Isle for a bunch of camping supplies. It listed something else that made me whoop: "Fogg 555-6917."

We loaded all the garbage into the boat and rode against the wind back to The Island. The clouds matted together like dirty cotton, blocking off the mountains. Static filled the air. Rebecca trembled, huddling under my arm as we hurried up to the Chutes' cottage.

Grampy and Mrs. Chute sat in the living room, drinking coffee and watching the fire dance. Rebecca ran to Grampy and held out her discovery. "Look what we found!"

Grampy's eyes gleamed as he looked at the fizzled rocket. "We'll get them rascals. Ooooo-ee!"

"And this," I said, handing him the crumpled receipt.

"Well, there!" said Mrs. Chute, leaning to read with Grampy. "I guess you have your proof."

"I guess prob'ly!" I said.

"Now can we do something fun?" said Rebecca.

"Well," drawled Grampy, "we could have a storytelling hour."

"Gee, I don't know," said Mrs. Chute, looking straight at him. "Nobody here likes to tell stories."

"Well, this is true, but I'd be willing to make the sacrifice," said Grampy.

Everyone laughed. Grampy even told tall tales about telling tall tales!

"So, what kind of story should it be?" Grampy propped his legs up on a stool and leaned way back in the rocking chair.

"Hackwax, Hackwax!" cried Rebecca.

"Yeah, old Chief What's-his-name," I said.

"Old Chief Hackwithax? In this weather? I really couldn't. It would be scary. Something awful! True story, you know." He made us beg for the story, and he loved every second of it. "Well, if you insist," he said after the tenth "Oh, please." "But if you don't get to sleep tonight, don't blame me!"

"We'll sleep fine," I scoffed. We'd be lucky if his story didn't put us to sleep.

Grampy made a horrible sound clearing his throat before he started. Now, that was scary.

"Way back before white folks found Fish Lake, the Abnakis lived on these shores, and their greatest chief was Hackwithax. He stood, oh, as high as this cabin." Grampy looked way up at a log rafter. "And he carried a tomahawk as big as a rifle."

"Who was Tom Hawk?" Rebecca wanted to know.

"Tomahawk, deah. It's a small ax that was used—"

"To scalp little blond girls with!" I jumped toward Rebecca and yanked her ponytail. She screamed.

"—to chop small trees and to skin game," Grampy went on, ignoring me. "Chief Hack-withax had a clever wife named Moaning Wind, and they were very happy together—until tragedy struck, the day Moaning Wind canoed to an island for berries to pick and dry for the winter." He sighed unhappily. A good act.

"Blueberry Island!" Dale said.

"Ayuh." Grampy pulled his empty pipe from his pocket and looked into the bowl before placing the stem in his mouth. He sure had his timing down. The suspense was keeping me awake.

"The wind was fetching thunderclouds ovuh the mountains, but Moaning Wind was too intent on her task to fret about the approaching storm. While she picked many baskets of berries, the wind doubled and tripled."

"Like today," said Rebecca.

"Ayuh. Only that day the wind carried in the worst hurricane these parts ever seen. The clouds broke, pouring down hailstones like hard-boiled eggs. Lightning flashed and wind bent the trees double—why, the white birches still lean ovuh Fish Lake to this day."

"I always wondered why they did that," Dale said.

I almost fell for it, too, until I did some figuring. Those birch trees would have to be hundreds of years old if that storm happened long before white folks found Fish Lake. I smiled to my Ellery-Queeny self. Grampy was probably making up this true story as he went along!

"Moaning Wind was a strong canoer and headed back to camp during a lull in the storm. At least, that's what they say, but nobody knows for sure because"—Grampy took a good long pause to look at each of us—"Moaning Wind nevuh made it home."

The Chutes and Rebecca oohed and ahed. Grampy went on, quiet and sad: "When Moaning Wind didn't come home, Hackwithax worried and went a-looking. Even the greatest chief of all struggled to steer the canoe through the treacherous waters. He, too, nevuh made it home."

Grampy stared into the fire, looking absolutely grief-stricken, the way Daddy does when he stares at the picture of Grammy. Everyone stayed quiet for a moment.

"Bah," I said, "that's not scary. It's a corny love story." Well, I should have known he'd drag it out.

"Let me finish," Grampy warned, lifting his wiry eyebrows. "Chief Hackwithax and Moaning Wind didn't make it back alive, but I know for a fact that their spirits haunt the shores of this lake." The way his eyes bugged out gave me the creepy-crawlies.

"How do you know?" asked Dale, right into it. If I'd said "Boo," he'd have hit his head on the Hackwithax-high ceiling.

Rebecca leaped up onto Grampy's bony knees. "I'm scared!"

"Don't be. There's no such thing as ghosts," I said, even though I have to admit to a slight belief in them after sunset.

"Listen," said Grampy. "You can heah Hackwithax now, if you try. He returns to search for his lost wife every time the wind and rain come together. Heah him?"

Nobody in the cabin made a sound.

"Yes, yes, heah this?" cried Grampy. "Mooo-aaannnnniiinnng Wiiinnnd, Moooaaannniiinnng Wiiinnnd. That's him, all right."

I tipped toward the window to listen and almost confessed to hearing it, but my common sense saved me. "It *is* the wind," I said, disgusted.

"Of course the wind is *carrying* the cry of Chief Hackwithax, Timothea. But you don't have to believe your ears. Believe me. I've seen him with my own two eyes." His eyes opened so wide, he looked like he was seeing a ghost.

Not that I actually believed him, but I had to ask, "Where? What happened?"

"On the shoreline back to camp. Took a swipe at me with that tomahawk and chopped my beard half off. Still got the scar. See?" He pulled part of his beard aside. There was a bald spot on his chin.

All right, he had me convinced.

Right then the sky exploded with thunder. Torrents of rain hit the roof. Everyone jumped and let out a howl of surprise, except Grampy. He just sighed, getting up, and said, "Guess it's about time."

"You really oughtn't cross the lake in this weather," said Mrs. Chute. "Please stay the night here?"

"Thanks, but I've made it through worse storms than this, my friend," said Grampy.

"Right, I bet Moaning Wind said the same thing when she headed for camp," I said.

"Hope you ain't a ghost next time I see you," said Dale.

Mrs. Chute wouldn't let us out the door until she got us wrapped up like sandwiches. Rebecca had on one of Dale's sweatshirts and his raincoat. I had on another of Dale's sweatshirts and Mrs. Chute's raincoat. Grampy had on Mrs. Chute's sweatshirt and two garbage bags she taped into a hooded poncho. He looked so funny, Rebecca and I couldn't stop giggling as we slipped and slid down the hill.

When Grampy's flashlight beam hit the trash floating around the boat floor in an inch of water, he grimaced. "You didn't tell me you brought home *all* the evidence!"

"I forgot," I said, which I had, carried away with Grampy's story and the storm. "We couldn't leave the glass and metal on the island, Grampy. What if an animal dug it up and got hurt?"

"Yeah, and plastic never decomposes," said Rebecca.

"Everything we ever needed to know about garbage, we learned in kindergarten," I said.

He patted our backs. "You did the right thing, girls." It felt good, making Grampy proud like that.

An Abnaki the length of a canoe was chasing me. He flailed an ax with a baseball bat for a handle. He caught me, ripped off my baseball cap, grabbed my ponytail, and wound up his bat-tomahawk to scalp me. Just as the ax swung, I twisted my head and screamed—for I saw it was a Paul Bunyan–sized Buddy Loring. He waved my scalped ponytail in my face and started hooting and hollering like when he hit the homer off me in last year's Independence Tourney.

The worst part was that I had a bald spot on the back of my head. The best part was that seeing the back of my own head didn't make any sense,

117

so I figured out it was a nightmare and woke myself up.

After I was awake, the hooting and hollering kept coming from outside, and Rebecca came screaming under my covers. "It's Hackwax!" she wailed, shaking and wheezing away. You couldn't blame her for being terrified. That noise cut through the wind and rain—loud, eerie, human and inhuman at the same time, just like an Abnaki ghost ought to sound: "HOOhooHOO-HOOHOO-hoo-HOOOOO!"

I leaned over to snatch Rebecca's inhaler off the dresser, then ducked under the covers with her. As she puffed, I prayed that Hackwithax wouldn't burst down our door. Finally the hooting stopped, but Rebecca was still scared, so I let her sleep with me, just so she wouldn't be alone.

As soon as the early birds started chirping, I peeked out the window. I half expected to see old Chiefie staring me in the face, but all I saw was fog and mist. The main camp was a shadowy lump at the end of the path.

Rebecca and I got dressed and sprinted through the fog and rain to the kitchen door.

Grampy's snores crackled out of his bedroom, and the floor trembled beneath my bare feet. "Is there a lawn mower in here?" I said.

Rebecca ran into Grampy's room before I could stop her. "Grampy, we heard Hackwax!"

He snorted awake. "Huh? Wha'? What's going on?" He drifted into the kitchen, coughing and trying to pull on a plaid flannel robe. He didn't have much luck moving, with Rebecca's arms locked around his waist.

"Did you hear Hackwax?" Rebecca mumbled into his T-shirt.

"What? Oh, of course. I told you, Chief Hackwithax always calls for Moaning Wind when—"

"No, Grampy," I cut in. "We heard this Abnaki war yell that sent chills up my . . . sister's spine."

Grampy rubbed his forehead with the back of his hand. "Well, I'll be jiggered. What could that noise be?" Suddenly he clapped his hands together. "I got it! Did it sound like this?" He gave a bloodcurdling yell, just like the ghost's: "HOOhooHOO-HOOHOO-hoo-HOOOOO!"

Screaming, Rebecca unlocked Grampy and glued herself around me.

I shook my head. I should have known the

noise was too scary to be true. The things that scare me the most never turn out to be true, like when Samantha and Lydia and I had a seance. We got scared out of our Reeboks because the one-and-only Elvis spoke with us from another dimension. Then we heard my father giggling behind the couch. Actually, the things that scare me the most usually turn out to be my father.

"Pleased to meet you, Hackwax," I said, holding my hand out for Grampy to shake.

"You think I—? Me, the ghost? Ha! It would have been clever, but no, that's the hoot of the barred owl. I've heard it many a time. Never in a storm, however." Grampy fingered the bald spot in his beard and lifted his eyebrows at us.

"But don't worry. If this storm keeps up, you just might run into the chief."

10

*T*he storm did keep up. The porch was so cold and damp that we spent the morning inside, a fire crackling in the living-room fireplace. Watching a fire is fascinating—for about five minutes. Boredom attacked me like a case of poison ivy, so I moved the grass-and-sky puzzle into the living room. It went together slowly because I couldn't keep my eyes off the door. Mama and Daddy were supposed to be back any minute.

Later in the morning, I let Grampy show me how to make his sourdough bread since he was making it anyway. While I kneaded the dough, Grampy bent over coughing. He'd been hacking away even more than usual all morning. He sounded so sick, I was worried about his plumbing and wiring.

Rebecca looked up from the tiny piece of bread dough she was molding into a frog. "Do you have a cold, Grampy?"

"Must be the weathuh." Grampy smiled with half his mouth.

I patted the dough ball. "Maybe it's bronchitis." Mama had that one winter, with a cough that wracked her whole body.

"Oh, I doubt if it's nothing like that," Grampy said. He set the bread dough to rising, then grabbed his yellow slicker from a hook next to the door. "Well, I've had enough of this rainy-day business. You two ready?"

"Ready to what?" I could just see him yelling up to the sky, telling Mother Nature to quit the jackassery.

"To pay the papuh company a little visit."

Rebecca and I ran to the bunkhouse for the rocket, the receipt, and our raincoats, then dashed ahead of Grampy to the Jeep. The rain gonged on the metal roof. When Grampy got in, water streamed off his slicker.

"Well, let's go," he said. The Jeep sputtered and skidded backward. Dirt clods slapped the rear window.

The Road had turned from dust to mud. Around the bend from camp, Grampy slammed on the brakes, and we slid to a stop. The beaver pond had become a river. Water rushed across the road, carrying sticks and leaves along.

"Jiminy Jehoshafat," said Grampy. "We'll never make it through that."

"What about Mama and Daddy?" asked Rebecca, her bottom lip quivering.

"They won't be getting here today on this road. But don't worry. They'll find a place to stay out to town." Grampy reversed the Jeep to Camp Timothea, and we slipped back downhill to watch the bread rise.

Funny, how that day passed quicker once I knew Mama and Daddy wouldn't be coming. I settled into the slowness of the afternoon, reading my July *Ellery Queen* for the third time and playing games with Rebecca and Grampy until his fingers got tired. He liked Clue—tittered like a hyena when he got Colonel Mustard in the parlor with a wrench.

For dinner we had bread, hot from the oven, slathered with butter and strawberry jam. Talk about melt in your mouth! After that, Grampy told us some more tall tales. *Stretched* tall. I'd have to be there to believe Daddy actually dated three girls in one night, and none of them found out about each other. While Grampy talked, I finished my puzzle. Well, almost. A piece of sky was missing.

"Yessuh, I knew you wouldn't get that puzzle all togethuh," Grampy said, grinning.

When pitch black took over the sky, Rebecca and I walked through the wind and rain to the bunkhouse. We had turned off the gaslights and settled into bed when Grampy came to the door.

"How you girls doing?" he said. I couldn't see him, not even a shadow, because it was so dark outside.

"Fine," I said. "What's up, Grampy?" He hadn't checked on us the other nights.

"Thought I'd stay out here tonight so that old barred owl won't frighten you again."

"Yay!" squealed Rebecca. She was really getting to like Grampy.

"Just try not to snore," I mumbled. "You'll keep the old barred owl awake."

Grampy laughed as he rustled under the bed

covers. Then, nonchalantly, he said, "Saw Hackwithax on my way here."

"What?" I grunted, halfway to neverland.

"Said I saw Hackwithax on my way to the bunkhouse."

My heart raced. "Really." I tried to sound sarcastic.

"Actually, I saw him following you girls out here."

Rebecca screeched.

"Did I scare you?" Grampy asked. "It is awfully dark outside. Maybe it was just a shadow. Good-night, girls."

"G'night," we said.

Grampy didn't speak for a while. I lay listening to the wind moan. Something thumped against the cabin.

"Timothea! Hear that?" Grampy whispered loudly.

"A—a—a tree branch," I said. "That's all it was."

"You're prob'ly right."

As soon as I started drifting off again, the bunkhouse door burst open and crashed against the wall. I was sure there had to be an ax behind it. Screaming, I leaped down from my bunk and pounced onto Grampy's bed. Rebecca, screaming too, scrunched into a ball under the covers at the foot of her bed. Of course, I didn't see that until Grampy turned on the gaslight.

I also didn't see the big grin on his face until then. He cackled and guffawed and slapped his legs.

"What's so funny!" I tried to keep the quivers out of my voice. Being scared witless has a way of shaking up your vocal cords.

Grampy handed me the end of a heavy fish line. "Reel this in," he said between tee-hees. "Here's your ghost."

I pulled the string taut. The door came away from the wall.

"You attached that line to the door handle! Grampy! You—you jackanapes!"

Rebecca moled her way out of her covers. "Grampy's the ghost?" I couldn't believe it, but she giggled.

"Timothea, dear, please get aholt of yourself," Grampy said. "It was just a practical joke. I didn't mean—oh—I'm so sorry! I thought you'd get a kick out of it, once you knew."

All of my sour feelings about Grampy flooded into my head. I remembered the unanswered letters, the years of not knowing him, the secret history of him and Daddy.

"You must really hate me!"

"Hate you?" Grampy looked dumbfounded.

"You've never cared about us. I don't know why you asked us here, but I know now why Daddy left you!" I just couldn't stand it in that bunkhouse another second. I ran to the dark camp. Grampy's voice chased me, a murmur in the wind.

With a flashlight from the kitchen, I went to the last place Grampy would look for me—his bedroom. The sharp apple smell of his pipe tobacco drenched me as I pulled the curtains shut. I paced back and forth, making and tracing a U around the king-sized bed. The flashlight cut a narrow beam into the coal darkness.

The beam flickered across the photo album resting on Grampy's rolltop desk. For something to do, I sat down and flipped the album open. The boy in the old black-and-white picture stared up at me from the circle the flashlight made. Grampy, with sparkling eyes, looked ready to spring a story. Avoiding that picture, I skipped to the back of the album.

That's when I found the letters. My letters.

They were held in a bunch with a rubber band. I stared down at the first-grade printing on the top envelope a long time before I stretched the rubber band off and shuffled through the pile. On each envelope the handwriting got nicer and smaller. I didn't look at the letters inside. I didn't need to.

On my last envelope, written when I was almost ten, the cursive letters in *Mr. James Lafler* looped just right. But there were other envelopes in the stack, three of them, unopened, addressed in shaky penmanship:

Miss Timothea Lafler
12 Winter Street
Scranton, PA 18510

Each envelope had a message stamped in red—
NOT ACCEPTED AT THIS ADDRESS. But the address was right! I've lived there all my life.

I wanted more than anything to read those

three letters. But they were in Grampy's room. I wasn't thrilled the time Buddy Loring sneaked into my room and pawed through my things. But this was different. Those letters were addressed to me. I carefully opened the first envelope and unfolded the plain paper.

—

Dear Timothea,

I just got your letter. I am so glad you are learning to write! First grade must be very exciting. Your father liked gym class best, too.

Thank you for inviting me to visit. It sure was nice seeing you a few months ago. I guess I will not be able to come back again until your parents invite me, though. I hope you understand.

Meanwhile, I hope you will come to see me at camp. The lake is beautiful. You will love it.

Write soon. I promise I will write back.

Forever yours,
Grampy Lafler

P.S. Say hello to your baby sister for me. Is she sitting up yet? Does she have any teeth?

—

I stared at the letter, wondering what had happened. Why had it been returned to Grampy? Lydia's grandparents were always dropping by as a surprise. Why did he need an invitation to visit us? Why, why, why? I tore into the other envelopes, looking for answers.

Dear Timothea,

Thank you for the nice letter. I am sorry you had to beg me to write back, but the oddest thing happened. I did write back to you, but the letter was returned to me. I double-checked the address, and it was right! Well, stranger things than that have happened to me before, like the time—well, I will tell you that story when I see you.

I am glad you finished first grade. Hurray for you! I wish I could shake your hand.

Thank you for inviting me to visit you and your sister. I would like to, but maybe it is best that I do not. Maybe someday your folks will bring you here to Fish Lake to see me. The reason for putting the lake on earth is easy to see. It is beautiful! But for now, what do you say we keep visiting each other with pen and paper?

I sure hope you get this letter, Timothea. I look forward to hearing from you soon.

Love,

Grampy

P.S. How is Rebecca? Is she walking?

———

Dear Timothea,

It sounds as if you are a bit miffed at me for not writing back to you. I cannot blame you. The thing is, I did write back to you twice, but both letters got returned to me for some reason. Well, I sure hope you receive this one. Three strikes and you are out.

I am glad you are doing so well in second grade. Now, now, do not get all huffy about having to do easy math homework. You do not mind having to practice hitting a baseball, do you? Sometimes it is hard to figure out the reason for putting up with things you do not like. But most things have a reason, if only you stop to figure it out.

No, I am afraid I will not be visiting soon. Perhaps you could come see me sometime? Charlie would love to see you. He misses you as much as you miss him! You should see his tail go when I show him your school *picture. Thank you for sending it to us. (Can you send us a picture of Rebecca, too?)*

Loving you always,

Grampy

P.S. How is Rebecca feeling? Are her allergies better now? Does she say "Dada"? That was your father's first word.

———

By the time I reached the end of those letters, my eye geysers had spouted up again. My insides felt . . . well, how do you even begin explaining feelings you can't figure out? I was all mixed up. Grampy *had* written back to me! He *had* cared about me after all! But why hadn't the letters been "accepted"?

Only one answer made any sense at all. I didn't get those letters because Daddy and Mama didn't want me to. And Grampy knew it the whole time. For two great parents to let a kid grow up not knowing a grandfather who cares about her, and for him to let it happen, there had to be something terribly wrong. I'd always suspected there was some awful secret my family had hidden quietly away from me. What was so horrible about Grampy that my parents didn't want him around? And what had changed their minds enough for them to leave Rebecca and me alone with him now? The mystery was like that grass-and-sky puzzle—it wouldn't come together because a piece was missing.

The puzzle made me want to scream until the sky cracked. I tore those letters in two and ran out of the camp.

_11

I was drawn to the shore. The rain, plopping on the lake, invited me to dive in. Behind me the lights blazed on in the camp. I heard Grampy calling me, anger booming in his voice.

"Timothea Lafler, this ain't hide-'n'-seek. Get yourself back. . . . " Hide-'n'-seek. It sounded like *hiding secrets.*

I had to get away. Blueberry was a distant black shadow on the water. I'd motor there in the dinghy to spite Grampy's rule (no motor) and his punishment (no boat). I grabbed the red blanket and a life vest from the speedboat, then got into the half-sunken dinghy. Rainwater lapped my shins. I got out and grabbed the giant tomato-soup can from the garbage pile still drowning in the speedboat.

Back in the dinghy, the storm plastering my hair against my forehead, I frantically baled the water down to a couple inches. Then I choked the motor and pulled the cord. It took a few tries before the motor coughed to a start. Grampy would hear that, but I was glad. "So there," that boat motor would tell him. "Who needs you."

Suddenly—I don't know why—memories poured into my mind, fuzzy like scenes from a very old movie. . . .

As soon as I stepped off the bus from kindergarten, I heard a deep voice hollering slurry words in the kitchen. I ran up the driveway.

Daddy was waiting in the doorway and scooched so I could run straight into a hug. Mama sat at the kitchen table, nursing Rebecca. A thin man, old, with sunken-in, unshaven cheeks, leaned against the counter. Charlie sat drumming the floor with his tail stub.

"Timothea! Give Grampy a hug!" Grinning, the man lunged toward me, and I ran to huddle under Mama's arm.

Grampy fell flat on his face.

Mama jolted and gasped. The baby cried.

Daddy hurried to help Grampy up. "Come on, Father. You've had a long day. Better sleep it off." Grampy didn't say anything else, just stumbled off to the family-room couch, leaning on Daddy.

The next morning when I woke up, I lay in bed listening to the voices in the kitchen.

"I'm some awful sorry about yestuhday," said Grampy. "I don't know what got into me."

Daddy made a laughy sound through his nose. "Same thing that always *gets into* you."

"What's wrong with a little celebration? It's not every day a new Lafler comes into the world. And if you hadn't moved so far away—"

"Hold it right there, Father. Our living in Scranton is not the problem. You know very well what the real problem is." Daddy's voice came out like oatmeal, all sticky and trying to stay in the saucepan.

I smelled tobacco smoke in the pause before Grampy spoke. "You lookaheah," he said, "I don't do nothing the rest of the world don't do. And I don't have to sit heah taking sass from my own son." A chair scraped the floor.

"Fine," Daddy yelled, "have it your way. Kathy and I have a family to raise. We don't need to be under your influence."

The door slammed.

With the motor at full speed, the little boat bulldozed through the waves to Blueberry, my dug-up memory replaying over and over. I tied the boat to a tree, then headed for the clearing to build a tent of pine boughs. The rest of the area was drenched, but the clearing just looked dewy. The tree canopy had kept out most of the rain.

While shining the flashlight around to find the driest spot to make camp, I smelled smoke. Wisps of it sailed by on the wind, spooky in the flash-light beam. I followed the smoke trail back to a maple where a red cave had burned into the roots, flames dancing higher with every blast of wind.

No time to think. Prop the flashlight against a rock to light the way. Run to the boat. Grab the tomato-soup can, fill it with water, race back to the tree to splash the fire.

It sizzled and steamed, but kept burning strong. I ran for water again and again. On my third trip to the beach, Grampy and Rebecca were there in the big boat.

"Don't just sit there," I screamed, filling the can and heading toward the clearing. "Help me put out the fire!"

On my next trip for more water I passed a shadow that was Rebecca running to the clearing with two beer bottles. "It's the tree next to the flashlight," I called. Grampy jogged by me with two more bottles.

After dumping his water, Grampy sat on a rock, coughing and struggling for air. Rebecca and I continued until at last only steam flitted from the maple. Exhausted, I wiped my hand across my forehead and leaned against the rescued tree.

Wind gusted through the clearing. Trees sprinkled water down like a dog shaking itself after a bath. The shower felt good against my face.

Then I remembered why I was there. Had Grampy found the letters ripped? NOT ACCEPTED AT THIS ADDRESS. "Cripes, how could that happen?" I muttered to myself, bitterness climbing up my throat.

"Well, I'd say the fire moved through the tree roots," Grampy said. He got up for the flashlight and traced the beam along the ground.

Mama helped me write to Grampy. She wouldn't have stopped him from writing back. Daddy must have had the post office return those letters. But why?

"See? Them roots go—or used to—right under that camp-fire spot, where it got so hot that the roots caught fire underground. But they didn't burn fast because fire needs air."

Because he didn't want me to get close to Grampy. Why? What caused the fight between them? What did Grampy do wrong?

"The fire gradually worked its way to the trunk of the tree, and took off when the wind picked up."

That time when Rebecca was newborn, what were Daddy and Grampy arguing about? Grampy acted weird, like the three kiss-the-cook jerks at the picnic, as if he was—

Drunk. Suddenly the past pieced together with the present, like a puzzle coming together after the grass and sky are in. No wonder Daddy had told me to steer clear and keep a level head if there was any drinking on the lake. No wonder the guys in Portage had laughed when they offered Grampy a drink and he said he didn't touch the stuff. No wonder. . . . My grandfather used to be a drinker.

Grampy nodded in the shadows. "If you hadn't come heah, Timothea, every living thing on the island could have burned. Now, don't you think you deserve a comfortable night's sleep back at the bunkhouse? We can talk in the morning . . . about anything you want to know." He sounded tired and defeated, as if he'd given up a hard struggle.

It struck me then that Grampy wasn't mad at me for running away. He understood.

—

We rode back to camp in the garbage boat, hauling the dinghy behind. Rebecca was wheezing and didn't have her inhaler. She breathed better after she used it back at the bunkhouse. Then she snuggled into the double bed with Grampy as if he was Mama or Daddy. I wasn't ready for that, but I was happy for Rebecca. That's what I wanted when I was six.

"G'night again," I said, settling into my pillow. Grampy shut out the light.

"Hope you ain't still mad at me about that door joke," he whispered in the dark. "I guess 'twasn't as funny as I thought. I guess 'twasn't funny at all. Hope you know I don't hate you."

I'd forgotten about Grampy Hackwax. "It's okay," I said. "It would have been really funny if you'd done it to Buddy Loring." I laughed, imagining it.

"Buddy Loring?" Grampy probably had his eyebrows lifted up to the third wrinkle on his forehead.

"Timmi's boyfriend," said Rebecca.

I groaned. "Half right. Buddy's definitely a boy. And use your inhaler again," I said. "You sound like an overworked donkey." I heard her patter out of bed and paw around for the inhaler, huff in the spray, and bounce back into bed.

Grampy sighed. "Girls, I can't tell you how wonderful it is to be with you. I love you so!

Good-night." He seemed to have trouble choking those words out.

I love you so. All warm inside, heart outgrowing my chest—the feeling I had right then is easy to describe. Happiness. But even after that, it was not a happy night.

12

Rebecca's asthma kept getting worse until even her inhaler didn't help much, and we didn't know why. It couldn't be the smoke on Blueberry; she'd have been sicker sooner. She didn't have a cold. She'd been taking her medicine. It wasn't allergy season, and Mama had cleaned every speck of dust out of the bunkhouse. We didn't even let Charlie in with us, except when Grampy had him wake us up.

"You must be allergic to Grampy," I said. "He's the only thing different in here." I giggled from nervousness.

"What's Rebecca allergic to besides smoke, dust, wool, and dogs?" Grampy asked.

"Cats, feathers, pollen, penicill—"

"Eureka!" cried Grampy, grabbing his pillow out from under Rebecca's head. "Feathuhs. Heah's the culprit. I brought the blasted thing in with me."

Grampy stormed to the door and threw the pillow out into the rain. The night had grayed into morning, and the pines towered black against the sky. "There," he said. "That's that."

But the feathers had started something that wouldn't stop. Rebecca wheezed and wheezed. When she breathed like that, the only thing to do was get her to a hospital, and quick.

"Grampy, we *have* to get her to town. But the road!" Panic exploded like fireworks in my stomach. We'd never get Rebecca to town through that flood.

Grampy nodded, thinking. Then he clapped his hands like a gunshot. "The landing t'other side of the lake is closuh to town, way past the beavuh dam. Mrs. Chute keeps a car there, hides the spare keys in a tree so they're always handy."

We hurried to dress. Grampy cradled Rebecca in his arms and moved fast and surefooted down the trail. His strength was amazing. Something like that happened to me when I pitched twelve innings against Buddy Loring's team in last year's Independence Tourney. I was tired, but I wanted that game so bad—I was afraid of losing, and I knew it was up to me. Nobody else has ever struck out Buddy Loring. Don't ask me where those extra innings of pitching came from. Somewhere. But we ended up losing the game anyway.

Now Grampy had some extra strength coming from *somewhere*. Maybe he was afraid of losing, too. Losing Rebecca. I could survive losing a baseball tourney, but I couldn't stand the idea of losing my sister. I ran ahead and started the big boat.

Grampy kept Rebecca on his lap as he steered the boat away from the dock. For once she didn't ask how long until we got there, or any other question. She just leaned against Grampy, her chest heaving as she whistled out her breaths.

I squeezed about a week's worth of worrying into the few minutes it took us to tear through the waves to the landing. Grampy piggybacked Rebecca straight to a big white birch, pulled a key out of a knothole, and hurried to a dented old pickup truck.

The road, though slippery with mud, wasn't flooded. We drove and drove, silent except for Rebecca's breathing. Grampy seemed intent on driving, and worry shoved aside all the *whys* I'd been dying to ask him. At last we passed the Cow Path gate, the beach, and the ball field.

"We'll be to the hospital in Presque Isle soon," Grampy said, turning onto the highway. His wrinkles sank deeper than ever; the bags under his eyes sagged lower. He coughed long and hard and had to slow the truck to use his handkerchief. His knuckles, grasping the steering wheel, turned white. That extra strength had gone back to somewhere.

At the emergency room, they called Rebecca in right away, even before a toddler with a cut head. Grampy and I went with her. The doctor gave her a shot of adrenaline and made her breathe steamy medicine through a plastic pipe.

"She's responding quite well," he said afterward, "but we may have to admit her, Mr. Lafler, if her lungs don't clear up after the next round of treatment."

Grampy started to say something, but coughed instead.

The doctor looked worried. "Mind if I take a look at that handkerchief?" he said.

"Mind? Of course I mind. And you mind your own business," Grampy snapped, trying to hold back some more hacking, but it took over. This time he couldn't hide it. The handkerchief turned red with blood. I gasped.

"Could we step into the hall a moment, Mr. Lafler?" said the doctor, flashing a don't-worry smile at me and Rebecca.

Grampy shrugged as if to say, "Sorry, Charlie." The broken look in his eyes right then scared me. I'd been waiting forever for my grandfather—I couldn't lose him now.

"But Grampy!" I blurted. "Let the doctor help you!"

"I wish he could," said Grampy gently. "No one can replumb and rewire a used-up man."

The last puzzle piece was in place. Grampy's "typical old man stuff" last month in the hospital *was* something to get worked up about after all. He needed us to visit now, when he still had strength to set things right. What had Mama said? Tie the gift of his life up with a bow? My throat and eyes felt prickly, but I won against the tears.

"Just fix up Blue Eyes heah," Grampy told the doctor. "That's all I want."

I went to my grandfather, put my arms around him, and squeezed. It was the first time I'd ever hugged him. It felt good when he kissed the top of my head and hugged back.

"If you insist," the doctor said.

Another shot and breathing treatment later, he pronounced Rebecca's lungs "clear as a bellows." The three of us Laflers smiled at each other and snuggled into a big hug.

Outside, the sun blared between cloud puffs that floated off, letting the blue sky show. No more rain.

Grampy smiled. "Well, well. Let us go home."

"Ayuh," I said. "Let's. You know any good stories?"

That fish that got away from him and Daddy thirty years ago up Houlton way was twelve feet long, Grampy said. I told him he said ten feet the first time he started the story. He said he couldn't help it if his memory was off the first time.

___

Back at the bunkhouse, Grampy and Rebecca and I cuddled up in the double bed and went to sleep. That's where we were when Mama and Daddy came in. I woke up to Charlie licking my face, Daddy holding him there.

I wanted to smile. Would I be doing the same thing to my kids someday? But of course I had to say, "Oh, Daddy, gross!"

"You look comfortable," said Mama, looking surprised.

"Slugabeds," said Daddy. Chip off the old block, Daddy.

Dale stood in the doorway, laughing. He must have brought Mama and Daddy in an Island boat.

"Where the tarnation you folks been any-ways?" Grampy asked, hitching himself up to sit against the headboard. "I waited suppuh for you." He made sure Rebecca and I saw him wink.

"Well, The Road's flooded out at the beaver dam. We had to stay in town last night," Daddy explained. "We CB radioed The Island and—" Daddy finally noticed the grin on Grampy's face. "Bosh, you know how we got here," he said.

"I've been here five minutes, and no hugs?" said Mama.

149

Rebecca ran to her then. I got up and hugged her, kind of shrugging at Dale over Mama's shoulder so he wouldn't get the wrong idea.

"What am I, a rock?" said Daddy. So Rebecca and I hugged him, too. That Grampy, he hopped up and gave Daddy a big, wet kiss on the cheek. We all had to laugh. Even Daddy.

I've read that an oyster makes a pearl by laying layer after layer of white to stop the itch of one little grain of sand. A secret gets covered up like that. But honesty grows like that, too—layer after layer of truth to stop the itch of the secret.

Grampy's letters were the itch. I had to know why Daddy had sent them back.

He thought he was protecting me, he said, and he hoped I'd never find out. "There's only one thing you can count on with an alcoholic: He'll always let you down," said Daddy. "I cut off contact with Grampy to keep you kids from getting hurt."

Grampy said alcoholics' families held the world's record for keeping secrets to protect each other.

150

I said, "Whoa, Daddy. How could a few letters hurt me!"

Well, it was a long answer. And didn't the stories come out then! True whoppers about the broken promises, the fights, the embarrassments caused by Grampy's drinking. It was hard for me to imagine him acting like those jackanapes at the ballpark, but he insisted he'd behaved even worse on many occasions. In fact, he'd even gone rabble-rousing with the Foggs in his barstool days, and they never let him forget it. The whole family had lived a warped life because of the disease—even Rebecca and I, if you count all those years of no grandfather.

Daddy couldn't recall one holiday or happy occasion that Grampy didn't celebrate into a disaster. When Rebecca was born, the proud grandfather had too much to celebrate on his way from Maine to Scranton. He showed up unexpectedly at the hospital and demanded to hold the baby. The nurses wouldn't hand her over, so he barged into the nursery to grab Rebecca out of the bassinet. He almost dropped her while pushing the nurses away.

"I decided it was better for you girls to have no grandfather at all than a drunk and dangerous one," Daddy said. "I didn't want your childhood to be like mine. That's why I returned those letters. And don't get mad at Mama, because I never told her," he finished.

"We'll fight about that later," said Mama.

Now that I knew some of the history Daddy was carrying around in his head, I understood why he'd tampered with the U.S. mail. But do good intentions set wrongs to right? I still don't know. In the end I forgave Daddy, though. After all, Grampy did, and he'd lost the most.

"The day I walked out of Jimbo's kitchen in Scranton, I drove straight to Northern Maine Medical Center to dry out. Took it one day at a time and ain't drunk a drop of hooch for six years," Grampy said. "On tough days I go to A.A. meetings—Alcoholics Anonymous. Went to one Saturday morning before the ball game, in fact."

Daddy looked flabbergasted. "Father! You really—? *That long ago?* Oh my lord. And I wouldn't listen until—"

"I know, I know," Grampy said, pushing out his arm to stop Daddy's words. "I read all about this sort of thing in *The A.A. Grapevine*."

How could I have missed *The A.A.* on the cover? The family secret had been exposed behind the toilet the whole time!

"See, it's normal for alcoholics' families to say 'No way, Jack' when the boozuh attempts to patch things up," Grampy explained. "It's not your fault. *I* was the boy who cried wolf. 'Quitting's the easiest thing in the world,' I used to say. 'I've done it a thousand times.' Well, it only counts once for an alcoholic.

"I thought whiskey was my friend," Grampy said. "The bottle was always there to listen to my troubles, to pat me on the back. Stabbed me in the back, too—time and time again. Losing time with my son and grandkids was the deepest stab of all."

He shined me that doting grandfather look of his. And this time I knew he'd always meant it.

The second week at Fish Lake was a real vacation. Daddy and Grampy and I went fishing

153

every morning. We never caught the trout that got away, but we caught breakfast most days. One day it was frogs' legs.

Dale showed me some great canoeing strokes. I showed him how to throw a curveball. Portage needed a pitcher.

We reported the jackanapes to the paper company, and they promised to keep a warden on duty every Fourth of July weekend.

"We'll hold you to that," said Daddy. "We'll be coming to camp every July from now on."

"But—"

"The *second* week, Timmi."

Daddy and Mama offered to take the rest of the summer off from work so we could stay at camp with Grampy. He wouldn't hear of it. Then they begged him to come back to Scranton with us, but you know Grampy. Stubborn.

Grampy died in November. Dale's keeping Charlie for us.

I hung the grinning-boy picture of Grampy beside Grammy's in the hall. Sometimes I catch Daddy smiling back at him. I smile, too. Grampy wouldn't like me to cry, and I don't want to anyway, because I can't look at that grin of his without remembering the ghost of Fish Lake.

I've got my barred-owl impression almost as good as Grampy's. The next time Buddy Loring tries to steal second, he has a big surprise coming. He'll be scared stiff.